THE CAT WITH A HEADACHE

The Complete

Cases of Cellini Smith

1941–42

ROBERT REEVES

---

illustrations by Peter Kuhlhoff

cover by Milton Luros

BLACK MASK
2025

Table of Contents

The Flying Hearse

Cellini Smith knew why the old lady sat there so calmly as the airliner droned through the storm. She was dead! What he didn't know was that she had been murdered. If he had he might have concentrated more on the possibilities of a fat fee, instead of giving his undivided attention to the pleasanter problem of making the far from fat blonde who was hostess for both the quick and the dead in that flying morgue wagon.

1

Through the Ozone

THE PLANE DROPPED as it hit an air pocket, then leveled out and continued its southwesterly course for the city of the angels.

Cellini Smith opened one eye and found the sight that met it sufficiently lovely to warrant opening the other. The sight wore a meticulously-pressed blue uniform. The shirt, tie and overseas cap matched in a lighter shade of turquoise, and the pleated skirt, Cellini noted, was criminally long by two inches. The uniform may have been of masculine cut but it encased as feminine a form as any connoisseur could hope for.

Cellini's eyes traveled up to the natural blond hair and the pale, oval face. He smiled at the hostess and said: "I approve."

The moss-green eyes seemed to smile back but she didn't ask what it was he approved.

"Where are we, Miss Lyons?"

"Over California, Mr. Smith. The low pressure area is well behind us and it's clear sailing the rest of the way."

"When do we land?"

The hostess glanced at her wrist watch. "We should be at Burbank airport in fifty-five minutes. Shall I arrange for transportation into town for you?"

"Yes, please."

"Fine, Mr. Smith. Anything else I can do for you?"

"Uh-huh. If you're staying over in Los Angeles long enough,

She sat there, glass in hand, drunk to the ears. "Hello," she said. "Let's drink a toast to Tubby's murder."

you can have dinner with me."

The blond hair shook sideways. "I'm sorry, Mr. Smith. Company rules." She smiled regretfully and went forward.

Cellini Smith shrugged but then gave an audible groan as a box-shouldered man sitting two seats ahead heaved, put around and grinned at him. He was large, prosperous-looking and of the hearty backslapping school of behavior. He had been trying to engage Cellini in conversation since Chicago. Cellini listened glumly to the bluff, domineering voice.

"Well, well, old boy. So you're up and about, eh? Had a nice nap?"

Cellini Smith grunted an affirmative.

"Don't know how you were able to do it right through that storm. Me, I couldn't sleep a wink. Almost made me a nervous

wreck, ha-ha-ha. For a while I was sorry I didn't stay on at Salt Lake."

Cellini remained silent but the monologue continued relentlessly under a widening grin.

"You're the quiet kind, eh? But still waters, you know. I heard you before. Trying to date up the hostess, you rascal. Ha-ha-ha. But don't get me wrong. I don't blame you, mister. Not at all. That Margery Lyons is a nice kid, ha-ha-ha. Say, my name's Haring—David H. Haring." He paused expectantly.

Cellini said: "That's nice."

Haring frowned. "Nice? Oh you're trying to get rid of me, ha-ha-a! Admit it now. You want me to shut up."

Cellini Smith admitted it.

"Swell! I like frank people. And please don't think I'm hurt, friend. I don't hurt easy. You got to have a thick skin when you're in business, ha-ha-ha. Say, friend, you don't even know my business. I'll give you my card."

"Quick," said Cellini, "before you forget it."

"Ha-ha, you're a one. I'm opening a branch of our firm in L.A. The phone company'll have my number in a couple of days. Maybe I'll make some money off you yet." He laughed again, tossed a card over to Cellini and settled back in his seat.

CELLINI SMITH SIGHED with relief and looked around. Besides Mr. Haring and himself, there were but three other passengers. Directly across the aisle, sat an elderly woman, apparently asleep. A knitted shawl was draped around her neck and a lap robe around her feet. Further down, in seat number seven, a young lady with auburn hair stared moodily out of the window. Cellini could see the side of her face. It was set in hard, brooding lines and the lips were a narrow, tight strip. A crossword puzzle book had fallen from her lap into the aisle. And directly in front of her sat her husband or, at any rate, the man with whom she had boarded the plane. He was fat, roly-poly, with a bald, full moon atop his head.

Cellini yawned ostentatiously and beckoned to Margery Lyons as she emerged from the pilot's cabin.

"Bored, Mr. Smith? Would you care for a newspaper?"

He pointed to the crossword puzzle book lying in the aisle. "I was thinking you might try and borrow that for me."

"Gladly." The hostess moved down the aisle, spoke to the auburn-haired girl and was soon back with the book and a pencil.

"Thanks," he said, "but don't go away. I can never start these things. Help me get the first word." With that, he opened the book at random and, on the margin over one of the puzzles, wrote:

That old woman across the aisle from me is dead.

Margery Lyons leaned over Cellini Smith's shoulder and read the message. He could smell a faint though decidedly pleasant perfume. He waited for some shocked exclamation of surprise but it didn't come.

"I see," she said. "I guess we need a four-letter word for silence." Without turning to look at the passenger in question, she took the pencil from Cellini's hand and wrote rapidly:

We know it, Mr. Smith. We've been in contact with Burbank for the past ten minutes.

Cellini nodded, flipped a page and penciled in reply:

Smart girl. Do you also know that she's been murdered?

This time there was a muted exclamation of horror. She caught at the neck of her uniform and shook her head, as if to say that it was impossible. But Cellini nodded his insistence and picked up the pencil again:

I'm sure it's murder. You'd better wire Burbank.

Miss Lyons read the message, seemed to hesitate for a moment, then moved off. Cellini leaned back in his seat and closed his eyes. After a while, he picked up the card that still lay beside him. It read simply: *David H. Haring, Investments.*

He stared at the card and wondered how Mr. Haring knew that Miss Lyons first name was Margery.

IT WAS SOME forty minutes before Margery Lyons again neared Cellini Smith and the dead woman sitting opposite him.

Cellini handed her the pencil but she stiffened and put a warning finger to her lip as David Haring abruptly stood up and made for the rear door.

Haring gave them a conspiratorial wink. "Excuse please. The little boys' room calls, ha-ha-ha." For a bare instant, his hand rested on Miss Lyons' hip as he squeezed by her. "Cross words, eh? Me, I only believe in polite words, ha-ha. That's how to get along in business if—" The door closed behind him.

"The human phonograph," commented Cellini. "Well, Miss Lyons, did you tell them what I thought?"

She glanced anxiously toward the auburn-haired girl and

the roly-poly man down front. "Not so loud please. Yes, Mr. Smith, we've wired the airport of your opinion of this unfortunate thing. And, incidentally, thank you for not changing your seat. The other passengers might have noticed and we want to avoid any sort of panic."

"Don't mind it at all. I wish that Haring was in the same silent condition. What's her name?"

"I couldn't say, Mr. Smith."

"Then whistle it. Give or I'll get out and walk home."

"Well—it's Mrs. Bella Riddle."

"Who is she? What does she do?"

"I don't know, Mr. Smith. Please believe me."

"O.K." Cellini jerked a thumb at the roly-poly man. "Here's something else you may not know. That animated beer keg with the billiard-ball skull is known as Tubby Moore. He used to be a pretty big racketeer in L.A. Worked in numbers and lottery. I think he's washed up now."

Margery Lyons nodded. "Yes. We've just heard that from Burbank. The company started an immediate check on the passenger list when you said it looked—that it wasn't a natural death."

"Then I suppose you also know I'm a private detective."

"That, too." A faint smile passed over the vermilion lips. "And that you were once mixed up with rackets in New York yourself."

"Perhaps, but it happens I was right here when Mrs. Riddle was killed. I ought to be the best man for this job. Why not get the company to give me a chance at clearing it up?"

"Their men are working on it already, Mr. Smith. Maybe—"

"That's all right."

The back door opened. David Haring came out, clucked an apology as he squeezed past the hostess and sat down.

"You might as well cancel my transportation into town," said Cellini.

"Yes, Mr. Smith. Is there anything else?"

"That perfume you use. It's nice."

Miss Lyons stayed her reply for a moment as she studied him. She saw a man in his early thirties of a little above average height. His two dominating features were a slim, tapering body that seemed capable of taking a lot of punishment and a quick, crooked, ingratiating smile. She said: "Yes, I know my perfume is nice. My boy-friend keeps telling me so." She smiled conventionally and went forward again.

Cellini Smith lit a cigarette. David H. Haring chuckled aloud as he made some notes on a paper—no doubt in anticipation of profits to be made from the new office. Down front, Tubby Moore was reading a book and behind him the auburn-haired girl still stared motionlessly out of the window.

And Mrs. Bella Riddle still sat with the lap robe around her knees, her mouth slightly open, her head lolling against the corner made by the window and back rest. To the casual observer, she was just an old woman dozing after a tiring night.

However, as Cellini studied her, he looked not at her face but at the yellowed hands which lay on her lap. They were arrested in the act of reaching for the small, white pills that lay scattered on the robe. Unlike the face, the hands were not relaxed, and even in death they seemed to be searching for something among those tiny round tablets. The pills had been spilled from the phial that also lay on her lap. That small green bottle with the pharmacy label looked harmless enough, thought Cellini, but it had spelled death for the old woman.

A sign warning the passengers to adjust safety belts began to blink over the forward cabin. Margery Lyons went down the aisle to check the belts. She stopped at the dead woman and leaned over her. "Here, Mrs. Riddle. Let me help you with your belt. It fastens like this. There. That's fine. I hope you didn't let that storm worry you. You certainly don't look worried." She patted the lifeless shoulder briefly and moved on.

Cellini lit another cigarette. It certainly looked like murder, he thought, and, what was even more certain, he'd try to share in whatever gravy oozed from it. Times were too tough to pass up any chance at some pocket lettuce. Of course, the problem was to find the client. As the hostess had said, the airline had its own corps of private dicks who were probably ready to tail each passenger as soon as the plane landed. Furthermore, they'd be unlikely to select a man who was himself one of the four murder suspects. So it seemed that Tubby Moore was the best bet. With his reputation, thought Cellini grimly, he needed a peeper badly.

The plane began to circle the airfield and Tubby Moore went through the futile routine of stuffing cotton in his ears. Cellini checked his watch. It was precisely 8 A.M.

The ground rose up to meet them, the plane bounced, then taxied down the runway and stopped. Steps were rolled up and the aft cabin door pulled open. Tubby Moore waddled out, followed by the girl in seat number seven. Cellini stood up to follow David Haring but the investment man paused. He pointed to Mrs. Riddle. "Say, that old dame don't look so good! She looks sick!"

"Your looks will never win a beauty contest either," replied

Cellini. "Come on." He urged Haring ahead of him and then stepped out of the giant airliner after him.

CELLINI SMITH LOOKED searchingly toward the barrier, then frowned.

Two or three reporters, a plainclothes cop, a couple of worried-looking airport officials and the usual complement of rubbernecks—but no one who would possibly be awaiting the arrival of Bella Riddle. Something jarred. An old woman—a sick old woman at that—traveling alone from New York to Los Angeles, should, ordinarily, have been met by somebody. But then, murder wasn't ordinary.

A man, carrying a black doctor's bag, hurried into the plane. Cellini walked over to the heavy-set police dick.

Ira Haenigson—detective-sergeant of Homicide—pointed a blunt forefinger at Cellini. "Now look, Smith," he said without preamble, "I don't know what you got to do with the Bella Riddle business and I don't even know what it's about yet, but I do know you from away back—so don't try any of your Indian rope tricks on me."

"I'm glad to see you too, Haenigson."

The Homicide man grunted. He was a good, old-fashioned police dick who hated to go near any of these new-fangled crime laboratories. To him, the best lie detector was the rubber truncheon.

"Beat it, Smith," he said. "You're not horning in here. And you'd better be in your office this afternoon because I'll want to see you."

Cellini shrugged and moved off.

Tubby Moore and the girl with him were getting into a large, black sedan that was attended by a uniformed chauffeur and a beefy-looking individual in startling tweeds. Maybe Tubby was washed up but he certainly hadn't forgotten to salt away a Cadillac.

Then, as an unobtrusive man left the group of spectators and boarded a cab behind the black sedan, Cellini nodded to himself. They weren't going to grab them for immediate questioning and a lot of publicity. For the present, it seemed, they were just putting shadows on them.

Cellini watched another shadow pick up Haring and then his practised eyes found the one he wanted. He made for a mild little man who was trying very hard not to look at him.

"What's your name?" asked Cellini abruptly.

The man gave a start. "Burke. What's it to you?"

"O.K., Burke. You're supposed to tail me and—"

"What are you talkin' about?"

A porter brought Cellini his gladstone. He glanced at the Cadillac. Luggage was being piled on the trunk rack. He spoke urgently. "Drop it, Burke. I'm an old billiard drinker and I can spot a tail in a football stadium."

Burke seemed ready to weep. "Just because I'm little," he complained bitterly. "Why don't you leave me alone? You big guys always step over me."

"Now, now," consoled Cellini. "Be brave. Who are you working for? Munson's? Is that the agency the company got?"

"Yup. If I only had another four inches—"

"Use a sap," counseled Cellini. "That'll make up for four inches any day. But forget it now and come on. Since you're supposed to tail me, we can take the same cab."

Burke frowned. "That wouldn't be right."

"Why not? We'll split the fare. Come on."

Cellini and the protesting Burke boarded a taxi as the Cadillac and the cab behind it pulled out. They circled the parking area and headed for Ventura Boulevard.

"It ain't right," said Burke nervously.

"Stop beefing. You got me where I can't get away and that's all a shadow is supposed to do. Besides, we're both saving half the taxi fare."

"Look, Smith, just because I'm little, it don't mean I'm dumb. You're up to something. What we tailing Tubby Moore for?"

"I want to talk to him."

"He murdered the old dame, huh?" The little man's voice was casual.

"I wouldn't know. All I know is I want to be hired by him to prove that he didn't."

"But supposing he did?"

"Don't quibble, Burke. Don't quibble."

"Maybe you did it."

"Murdered Mrs. Riddle?" asked Cellini. "Sure, but wild horses couldn't drag a confession out of me. What does your outfit think of it?"

The shadow shrugged. "As soon as the plane radioed, the company hired our firm to investigate. They just give us the passenger list and I drew you to tail. I wish to hell I had to check on a guy smaller than me for once," he added morosely.

"Haven't they got any suspicions?"

Burke again made the characteristic shrug of his thin shoulders. "Even if they had, nobody'll tell me. Besides, it's not sure it was murder."

"O.K." Cellini Smith leaned over to the driver and indicated the black sedan. "I want to see somebody in that car."

The cab shot ahead, drew abreast of the Cadillac, then cut into the curb, forcing it to stop. Cellini waved to Burke and got out.

2

Tubby Moore

THE CHAUFFEUR WATCHED Cellini Smith through slitted eyes as he put one foot on the running-board. The beefy man in loud tweeds who sat next to the chauffeur was more truculent. A calloused hand leaped out and bunched Cellini's lapels in a tight grip.

"Now, now, Lou," said Tubby Moore mildly, "don't hit the gentleman till we know what he wants."

Cellini braced himself and his clenched knuckles smashed down on Lou's wrist. The guard's hand fell away with a yelp of pain.

" 'The wildest savag'ry, the vilest stroke,' " murmured Tubby Moore. "That's Shakespeare," he added.

"Tell your gorilla he'll need a credit dentist if he starts anything—and that's Cellini Smith."

"You seem a man of opinion, Mr. Smith, but what in"— he turned to the auburn-haired girl seated beside him—"… Excuse me, my dear… But what in hell do you want from me?"

"To talk to you for a few minutes—for your own good."

Tubby Moore considered it, reached over and pushed the rear car-door open. "Very well. Ginger, this gentleman says he's Cellini Smith—Mr. Smith, my wife."

The racketeer's wife said nothing. Pretty, thought Cellini— but so were pythons. She moved needlessly far as Cellini sat between them, the car gears meshed, and they sped toward

Hollywood.

Tubby Moore inserted a grotesquely fat cigar between his puffy lips and carefully lit it before turning to Cellini. "If I remember correctly, Mr. Smith, you too came through from New York on that airliner, but what could you tell me that would do me any good?"

"Is your memory good enough to remember that old woman who sat opposite me?"

"Yes. The one who slept all morning."

"Only she wasn't sleeping. She was murdered."

Cellini silently cursed the rolls of insensate fat on Tubby's face. They made it the perfect poker face. Mrs. Ginger Moore, however, gave a sharp, hissing intake of breath and, in the front seat, Lou's mouth fell open in honest amazement.

"Well," asked Tubby Moore finally, "suppose she *was* murdered. What's it to me?"

"I'm a private dick and you need one badly, Tubby."

"I see." He essayed a smoke ring before continuing. "What makes you think I need a dick? And don't call me Tubby."

There was something about the fat, round face and the mild, velvet voice that made Cellini realize that Tubby Moore was a much more dangerous customer than he looked. He said: "You certainly need a dick, Tubby. Two cabs are following this car right now. One of them's tailing me but the other's tailing you."

Lou stared out the rear window for a moment, then gave a low whistle. "The guy's right, boss. They're tailing us."

" 'Foul whisperings are abroad,'" murmured Tubby Moore.

Cellini stirred impatiently. "I know. It's Shakespeare. But how about hiring me to get the murderer and put you in the clear?"

"You're being followed too," reminded Tubby Moore. "You need a dick as much as I do, Mr. Smith."

"I can take care of myself, Tubby. That's my business. Besides, you're the best candidate for the murder. You've got a police record that takes ten minutes to read. Don't forget you're a racketeer—or you were one before the cops stepped on you."

"For your information, Mr. Smith, I haven't retired yet. And as for me hiring you—no dice. That's final."

The car slithered to a stop.

"O.K., Tubby. I've got a hunch we'll see each other again." He opened the door.

"Go ahead, Lou," said the racketeer. The guard's sledge-hammer fist lashed out and connected with the nape of Cellini's neck. Cellini crashed down on the pavement.

Tubby Moore looked out the window as Cellini dazedly tried to gain his feet. "I told you not to call me Tubby," the mild voice said. An engaging of gears and the Cadillac shot ahead.

Cellini Smith stood up shakily. A thin smile appeared on his lips. There was no joy in it.

LITTLE BURKE COMPLAINED for the third time: "I don't know why you don't tell me what happened."

Cellini Smith made no reply. He stared with unseeing eyes at the ceiling of the cab. His brow was clouded with a black, unreasoning anger and his clenched fist trembled slightly.

"So Tubby Moore's gorilla ganged up on you and threw you out of the car," pursued Burke querulously. "So what? It happens to me every week but I don't get unsociable on account of it."

"He didn't throw me out."

"All right, he didn't throw you out. You were out and he didn't throw you in. All I want to know is what chance there is that Tubby Moore did the killing."

"A damned good chance," said Cellini grimly.

"What makes you think so?"

"Forget it."

The cab stopped in front of an antiquated office building that some realtor had once dared to call Spanish-style. Cellini stepped out. "I'm going up to my office," he told Burke. "Come on."

"No thanks. Think I'll run along."

Cellini's eyes widened. "I thought you were supposed to tail me."

"No, not really," said Burke evasively. "I mean I was only supposed to find out where you were going and then report back."

"O.K."

"Wait a second, Smith. Tell me why you think there's a damned good chance that Tubby Moore killed the old dame. Come on," he wheedled. "Pretty please."

"It's just something that happened in Salt Lake," said Cellini. "On account of the storm, Mrs. Bella Riddle decided to come the rest of the way by train. So did Tubby Moore. But when the passenger agent of the airline assured Mrs. Riddle there was no danger, she changed her mind and took the plane anyway. That's all."

"Where does Tubby Moore fit in?" asked the pint-sized Burke.

"The moment Mrs. Riddle decided to continue by plane so did Tubby...."

Cellini Smith pushed the door of his office open. The layers of dust on the furniture, the dust curls on the floor and the pile of letters were mute indications of his three week's absence.

However, it was with some pride that he sat down to his desk. As a result of his flying trip to New York, the office now belonged to him. He was a private op on his own.

He sat at his desk for a while, hesitating as he tossed mental coins. Did this death of an old and unbefriended woman warrant a long distance call to the Sampsel Agency in New York? If he was going to follow this thing at all, his one chance was to try and get a jump on the shams and hope to snag a client later. He dialed long distance and in five minutes the connection was completed.

He spoke rapidly, for the operator had instructions to sever the connection after three minutes. Bella Riddle, Cellini told Sampsel, was the subject. Every available item of information about her. Friends, family, background—everything. She had come through on the night plane from New York. Who saw her off? Where did she buy her ticket? What address did she give the ticket agent and who was to be notified in case of accident? And if anything important turned up, to phone back—otherwise to wire. But the important thing was speed…

The call completed, Cellini spent another half-hour sorting papers and checking the mail. Unpaid bills everyplace. They were a grim reminder of his urgent need for a client. He would make some sugar out of this Bella Riddle business he promised, and, what was equally urgent, he'd repay a little debt to Lou—that bodyguard of Tubby Moore's, who was so free with his hands. The jingle of the phone interrupted his thoughts.

"Yes?"

"This is Ginger Moore," said a husky, feminine voice.

"If you're worried about your darling husband," replied Cellini, "forget it. It's his playmate you should worry about."

"No, Mr. Smith, it's something else. I want to see you."

"O.K., but I'm busy for at least an hour."

"Then will you come as soon as you can, Mr. Smith?"

"Yes. Where is it?"

She supplied the address and he cradled the receiver. He was about to quit the office when he recollected Burke's coy evasiveness about shadowing him. He found a sheet of paper and wrote:

Burke:

When you case this office put everything back where it belongs and lock the door with the spring latch. If you touch the whiskey in the filing cabinet I'll break your neck.

C.S.

Then he left.

CELLINI SMITH PICKED up his car, an old, catarrhic Plymouth coupé, and in less than fifteen minutes parked before a squat, ugly building—the county morgue.

He walked down a sloping driveway and turned into a low-ceilinged office. "Hello, Pete," he said.

A shirt-sleeved man sitting at a desk swiveled around. "Times are tough, Smith. Five bucks will do it for you though."

Cellini selected a fin from his slender wallet. "You should have been a tree surgeon, Pete—you're a fine grafter. I want to know about Bella Riddle. Did she come in yet?"

"Twenty minutes ago. Just sent her up for a p.m."

"A post mortem already? That's quicker than usual, isn't it, Pete?" Cellini asked.

"They're rushing it to see if it's a homicide. There's some argument over jurisdiction."

"Uh-huh. Where are her things?"

Pete reached for a large manila envelope lying on his desk. "We sent her clothes up for examination but here's her pocketbook."

Cellini opened the envelope, took out a purse and spilled its contents over the desk. It contained the usual odds and ends of comb, powder puff, hair pins and other trivia. There were also nearly three hundred dollars in travelers' checks, some loose change, a ticket stub, a small snapshot of a henpecked-looking man and a plain, typewritten sheet which said simply:

Mrs. Riddle:

Enclosed is your ticket for Flight No. 6. Our Mr. Benson will meet you at the Burbank airport in California. We trust you will have a nice trip and that you will notify us of your new address.

There was no signature. But there wouldn't be, thought Cellini, because the author of that note had sent a woman to her death. And who was Mr. Benson? Why hadn't he met the plane?

From without, came the sound of voices and shuffling feet. Pete managed to scoop the purse and its contents back into the manila envelope in time as Detective-sergeant Haenigson and one of the airport officials entered.

"So you been peddling information to this Smith," grunted

Ira Haenigson.

Pete banged the desk in righteous wrath. "Listen, you pigeon-toed crime buster," he shouted, "you can't accuse me of taking graft!"

"Shut up, Pete. You'd sell your own grandmother to a glue factory." The Homicide man turned his baleful eyes on Cellini but his voice was surprisingly calm. "Smith, you're chasing your tail off for nothing. The doctor at the airport said that Mrs. Riddle died of heart failure because of the storm. The only reason they're doing a p.m. is because the law requires it."

Cellini said: "The p.m. will show that Bella Riddle was poisoned—by those pills on her lap."

The airport official whispered something to the detective-sergeant.

Haenigson indicated the door. "Beat it, Smith. Maybe I'll see you at your office this afternoon."

"Why maybe?"

"Because we only got your say-so she was murdered and because we don't know if she was already dead when the plane crossed the California border. The Nevada authorities are trying to get jurisdiction over the case."

Cellini thought of questions he could ask—of this Mr. Benson who didn't meet Bella Riddle, of the shadow's report on Haring, of other things—but he thought it wiser to get, while he could. This wrangle between the California and Nevada authorities gave him valuable time and he had a lot of things to do.

CELLINI SMITH SPED down Wilshire Boulevard to keep his appointment with Ginger Moore. He stopped at his office only long enough to find whether Burke had made the expected visit. Over Cellini's message, the little shadow had written his thanks for leaving the door open and his regrets over finding the office innocent of anything connected with Mrs. Bella Riddle. The whiskey bottle in the filing cabinet was emptier by three hookers which, thought Cellini, was more reasonable than he had anticipated.

The first of Sampsel's reports was also waiting in the office but the information in the telegram was meager. It seemed that Bella Riddle's airline ticket was bought with cash by an unknown person, that she had no family and that her husband, Herman, had died the year before. Also, Bella Riddle had supplied the airline with no name for notification purposes.

Cellini still mulled over these few items when, a few minutes later, Ginger Moore admitted him into the three-hundred-a-month apartment.

She had had the time to repair the ravages of the journey and, decided Cellini, she was even prettier than he had thought. The face and eyes, however, were hard and unfriendly. Not the kind of woman who cried easily.

"Where's Tubby?" he asked.

"He's out taking a bath."

"Does he always leave the house to take a bath?"

"A Turkish bath. It's down the block."

"He needs sweating. What did you want to talk to me about, Mrs. Moore?"

"That proposition you put my husband about working for him. Are you still willing to investigate the killing, Mr. Smith?"

Cellini nodded.

"Very well then. I'm willing to hire you."

Cellini tried not to show his elation. "All right, Mrs. Moore. It makes no difference to me which of you is my client."

She fumbled in her purse. "I haven't much money. I can give you a hundred dollar retainer right now and if you succeed I can give you another five hundred dollars. Is that sufficient?" she asked coolly.

Cellini counted the bills, then folded them into his wallet. He felt that his career as an independent private op was starting well. "More than enough, Mrs. Moore, but let's get it clear. You'll give me the other five hundred dollars if I can prove that your husband didn't kill Mrs. Bella Riddle."

"No, Mr. Smith, I don't mean that." The hard, unfriendly eyes seemed to look right through him. "I mean, Mr. Smith, that you'll get the other five hundred if you can prove that my husband *did* kill Mrs. Bella Riddle!"

Cellini blinked.

She said: "You heard correctly, Mr. Smith."

He stared at her, trying to discern some flicker of amusement, some sign of the practical joker in that hard face. But Ginger Moore was deadly earnest. "So you think he did the killing?" he finally asked.

"I don't know."

"Then how should I?"

"That's your business, Mr. Smith. That's what I'm hiring you to investigate. You'll admit that he has a very good chance of being the guilty one, won't you?"

"Perhaps— I don't know yet."

"Well, your job is to find out and see that he doesn't get away with it. That's all."

"You don't seem to be a very good example of the devoted

wife, Mrs. Moore."

For the first time she gave a thin smile. It wasn't pleasant. "That's aside from the matter."

"If it's like that," he pursued, "why don't you leave him?"

"If you knew Tubby Moore, Mr. Smith, you wouldn't ask. The only way I could ever leave him would be in a coffin. Him and Shakespeare! The point is: do you accept the job?"

"Uh-huh." He spoke slowly to emphasize each word. "But I won't frame Tubby."

"I haven't asked you to, Mr. Smith."

"Then it's set. Can you give me any lead to start on?"

She shook her head.

"Why did you and your husband go to New York?"

"I went because he went. I don't know his reason."

"In Salt Lake," stated Cellini, "you and your husband decided to finish the trip to L.A. by train, on account of the storm. Why did Tubby suddenly change his mind?"

"To find that out," said Mrs. Moore, "is why I gave you a hundred dollars."

3

Turn on the Heat

CELLINI SMITH FIRST stopped by his office to see there were more telegrams and to learn from the phone company whether any long distance call awaited him from Sampsel. He drew a blank on both counts. Twenty minutes later, he entered the *Supreme Turkish Baths*.

He surrendered his valuables for safekeeping to a man at the desk and, in exchange, received a locker key from which dangled an elastic, and a yellow bed sheet.

He was about to move on when the clerk said: "Are you Cellini Smith, sir?"

"Yes."

"Well, we hope you enjoy the baths, Mr. Smith. Please feel free to take full advantage of our facilities and to order anything you want—with the compliments of Mr. Moore."

Cellini nodded and walked down a flight of stairs into a long room lined with benches and numbered metal cabinets. He found the locker that corresponded to his key, undressed and put his clothes away. He did this last with some reluctance. If Tubby Moore was expecting him, he might need his clothes for a hasty departure. But it couldn't be avoided now, so he slipped the key onto his wrist, wrapped himself in the bed sheet and stepped through another door to find himself in the dank, vaporous atmosphere of the baths.

Some customers strode up and down in their sheets, looking

much like Roman senators, as they waited to cool off. Others, their flesh a lobster pink, scurried for the showers. A harassed orderly ran back and forth trying to service them with cool drinks, towels and other incidentals. Various doors led to a small gymnasium, the hot-room and the Russian steam-room. To one side of the room in which Cellini found himself, more customers lazed in hot, salt water baths that were sunk into the floor.

Tubby Moore was not to be seen.

Cellini brushed aside an athletic-looking individual in white trunks who tried to entice him into one of the salt water tubs and crossed to several curtained, canvas cubicles on the far side. Cautiously, keeping watchful eyes on the men around him, he inspected these cubicles.

He found his man in the last one, Tubby Moore was lying on his stomach, over a rubber-matted table, in all his porcine, naked glory. The while he grunted in agony, he squirmed with pleasure as a masseur kneaded the ample rolls of flesh.

"Oh," said Tubby. "You got here."

"That's right. I got here."

Tubby looked up at the large, musclebound masseur who was thrashing his arms around like a windmill. "Hiram, I think this man wants to gang up on me. Don't let him."

"No," said Hiram phlegmatically, "I won't let him do nothing like that."

"Don't worry," said Cellini, "It's your friend, Lou, I want—not you."

"Oh." The racketeer was very relieved. "Lou's not here. I don't know what your beef is anyway, Mr. Smith. I told you not to call me Tubby, so just forget the whole thing like a good boy and keep your morale up."

Cellini said, "Sure, Tubby," and lowered himself, morale and all, onto a bench. He watched the masseur pound and slap the jello thighs and marveled at the superfluity of flesh the racketeer had amassed. His stomach was large enough for two, his chin was in triplicate and those little pig-eyes with black, pinpoint irises had enough bags under them for a luggage shop. He wasn't a pretty sight.

"Lucky you're not in Germany," said Cellini. "They'd slaughter you for your fat content."

"So my wife told you where I was," Tubby Moore managed to emit between groans. "Ve-e-ry nice of her."

"Don't the two of you get on well?" asked Cellini.

"Well?" Tubby Moore took in air and delivered a high-pitched laugh. "She hates my guts—as you can see, that takes a lot of hating." Hiram worked his legs now and he could speak more freely.

"Then why don't you let your wife leave you, Tubby?"

"I wouldn't stop her, though she's kind of svelte and I like her in a way. But God, what a shrew she is! Did you ever read the *Taming of the Shrew?*" he asked of Hiram who now made and unmade ripples of flesh along his spine.

"I ain't got a library card," declared the masseur.

"The funny thing is," ruminated the racketeer, "that when I married her you couldn't imagine she'd turn into the termagant she is. She was so-o good. Wouldn't touch caviar because it had something to do with the sex life of a fish."

"Why did you go to New York?" asked Cellini.

"*Trees,* too," mused Tubby Moore.

"What are you talking about?"

"My wife. She used to sing *Trees.*" He shuddered.

CELLINI WATCHED WITH fascination as the fat body quivered and convulsed like a cooch dancer's under the electric vibrator that Hiram applied. "I still don't get it," he said. "If it's like that with your wife, why doesn't she pack up and leave?"

"She knows she wouldn't get a penny from me and she's not the kind who likes to work for a living. I like her though. Not like my first wife. The first one used to squeeze the candies in a box before choosing one she wanted."

"That is bad," agreed Cellini, "but I'd still like to know why you took this trip to New York."

"Business," said Tubby.

"I thought the police closed your business. The numbers racket is supposed to be through in this town."

"That doesn't mean I can't start a new business, Mr. Smith. Crime flourishes in this town like the green bay tree and I have every intention of cutting in on it again."

"Tubby, do you know anyone called Benson?"

"Don't think so. I've got a bad memory for names."

Tubby Moore sat up as the masseur finished with a final flurry of slaps on his stomach. "Very good, Hiram. You deserve a dollar tip for this."

"Thank you, Mr. Moore. That's swell." He noted the tip on a pad and then handed it to the racketeer for his initials. As Cellini watched the pencil course over the paper, he could see that it was something more than simply a set of initials.

Tubby returned the pad to the masseur. "Here. You can run up to the office with it now. You're all right, Hiram, except that you ought to catch up on your Shakespeare."

Hiram promised solemnly and left.

Tubby Moore wrapped a sheet around his blimp-like body. " 'And thus I clothe my naked villainy,' " he declaimed. "Well, are you coming along or taking a rub-down?"

"I'm here only to find out who killed Bella Riddles—not for rub-downs."

Tubby looked at the well-muscled shoulders and the V-shaped body with some envy. "I guess you don't need one anyway, Mr. Smith. How do you keep in such good condition?"

"It's a simple secret," confided Cellini. "Before breakfast, never drink whiskey unless it's bonded. Where to now?"

"The hot-room for exactly seven minutes." Tubby led the way past the salt water tubs till they reached a vapor-clouded, glass door. He pushed it open and stood aside for Cellini to pass through.

Tubby Moore was not a very observant man. He did not notice that instant of hesitation on Cellini's part nor the sudden tensing of his muscles under the sheet.

As Cellini walked into the hot haze he abruptly dropped to one knee as a hamlike fist whizzed harmlessly over his head. His arms shot out, tangled between a pair of ankles, and Lou came crashing down on the marble floor.

"God what a fool that Lou is," said Tubby Moore calmly. He carefully closed the door behind them as Lou stood up groggily and began weaving toward Cellini.

Cellini accepted a pawing, harmless blow on his shoulder. With cool, precision-like exactitude he drew a bead on Lou's wide mouth, then his knees bent slightly, his right shoulder swung back and his fist shot forward. The gorilla went down like an eyelid.

"A hit," cried Tubby Moore, "a palpable hit."

A thin, cadaverous man who sat sweating in a corner said: "I ain't taking sides. I got nothing to do with this. Leave me out."

Trickles of blood seeped from between Lou's cut lips and broken teeth. "I see what you meant about the credit dentist," remarked Tubby Moore.

Hiram appeared, took in the scene with his usual dispassion and half-carried, half-dragged the dazed gorilla out.

THEY SAT ON one of the many benches that lined the room. A hot, dry air poured down on them from vents in the ceiling. "You shouldn't have taken so long to sign your name when you gave Hiram that message," said Cellini.

"Eh?" Tubby's overlapping brows suddenly cleared. "Oh, I see. You're a good man, Mr. Smith. I hope you won't try to take it out on me for this."

"Not unless you start something."

"No fear. How about forgetting the detective business and working for me?"

Cellini shook his head.

"I could use you," continued the racketeer. "Lou is dumb enough to catch mice with. He used to be the worst free-hand forger west of the Alleghenies."

"Forget all that, Tubby, and listen to me. Early this morning when we landed in Salt Lake you decided to come in the rest of the way by train, didn't you?"

"That's right."

"Why did you change your mind and come by plane just when Bella Riddle changed her mind?"

"Are you trying to pin this killing on me, Mr. Smith?"

"Yes."

"Perish the thought," sighed Tubby Moore. "Smarter men than you have tried such things. And my wife's one of them."

"So that's how you guessed I'd be coming here? You knew your wife would hire me?"

"Sure," said Tubby. "I can read Ginger like a first grade primer. She's quite a crackpot but I like her."

"Maybe she wants to pin the killing on you because she thinks you did it."

"Mr. Smith, I've done a lot of mean things in my time but I don't go around killing defenseless old women."

The talking cadaver in the corner asked: "Are you a policeman, mister?"

"A private detective," replied Cellini.

"Really? I own a delicatessen."

"Go away," said Cellini. He turned to the racketeer again. "I still want to know why you changed your mind in Salt Lake and followed Bella Riddle."

"Not to murder her," was Tubby Moore's measured reply, "and if you want the truth, the only reason I changed my mind was because of shame. I figured that if an old woman wasn't afraid to continue the trip by plane, then I shouldn't be either."

Cellini made no reply. They sat there, sweating, for some moments before Tubby Moore broke the silence. "You don't look very convinced," he said shrewdly, "but why pick on me? I wasn't the only one on that plane. There was a man a couple of seats in front of you."

"That was David H. Haring. Do you know him?"

"Haring? Never saw him before or after." Tubby rose. "Come on, Mr. Smith. The seven minutes are up."

The cadaver called a good-bye after them and Tubby Moore led the way into the Russian steam-room. The walls were made of some thick, porous rock that was heated by concealed pipes. Ceiling nozzles sprayed steady streams of water over these walls to create a fog of hissing steam. Where, before, the heat had been dry and bearable, now it was humid and stifling and penetrated every fibre of a man's body.

Tubby Moore sank down on a slatted table in the middle of the room. The attendant in white trunks entered with what seemed to be a large feather duster and a pail of soapy water. He whipped the water into a lather, dunked the duster into it and began beating the feathers over Tubby's torso.

Cellini, vainly struggling for a deep breath, watched the operation. Tubby's arm hung loosely over the table and he noticed his locker key dangling from the pudgy wrist. He leaned forward. The number was *43-A*.

"I don't think I can take this any more," said Cellini quite truthfully and walked out.

Cellini Smith showered and dried himself, then went down to the lockers. He dressed slowly and, at an opportune moment, moved along the rows of lockers until he found *43-A*.

With one hand he pressed firmly in on the jamb facing the lock and with the other yanked sharply at the handle. It was an old trick. The twisted frame gave and the door opened.

Cellini Smith began his search of Tubby Moore's clothing with small hope. Not that he was convinced of Tubby's complete innocence—the racketeer had lied on certain points. It was simply that Tubby was too old a hand to forget any interesting items in his clothing. In addition, anything of importance was likely to be with his other valuables in the office.

Then it was that Cellini found it in the breast pocket of Tubby's herringbone jacket. It was one of David Haring's by now familiar business cards. And on its reverse was the penciled scrawl: *Bella Riddle.*

4

Playmates

IT WAS NEARING five in the afternoon when Cellini Smith returned to his office. Another telegram from Sampsel disclosed the pointless information that Bella Riddle was known as Bella Heffer prior to her marriage, that she had always been unwell and that once, in her youth, she gained some notoriety by hiccuping for nineteen days.

The afternoon papers, which Cellini had picked up, gave no hint of murder. The story, on inside pages, spoke only of the death of Mrs. Bella Riddle, age sixty-one, from heart failure aboard a transcontinental plane.

Cellini's next move was to make several phone calls to friends in the police department and the D.A.'s office. But nobody seemed posted on David Haring or the elusive Mr. Benson who should have met Bella Riddle at the airport.

Cellini sat behind his desk, chain-smoking with one hand and doodling on the desk blotter with the other as he considered the case. Obviously, Ginger Moore's desire to pin the killing on Tubby didn't stem from her alleged fear of leaving her husband or even from any particular hatred of him. More likely, if Tubby's fat body could be squeezed into an electric chair, the family bank account would become hers. Or was she merely trying to confuse issues—trying to conceal some guilty connection with the killing? And what of those other posers? What sort of unholy, three-cornered alliance existed between

Tubby Moore, David Haring and the deceased Bella Riddle? And why the familiarity that David Haring displayed toward Margery Lyons—the hostess with the heavenly figure?

Cellini's meditations terminated abruptly with the entrance of Ira Haenigson—the detective-sergeant.

"Listen, Smith, I been up here twice this afternoon. I thought I told you to stay put."

"I was taking a bath, Haenigson. I wanted to look my best for you. Sit down."

The Homicide man grunted and chose a chair with care—as if expecting some April Fool's trick. "How come you went to New York, Smith?"

"I went because Sampsel wasn't satisfied with the dough coming out of his west coast office here. We had a fight and called off the partnership and now I own this office lock, stock and red ink. Has it been settled where Bella Riddle died?"

"In California ozone, Smith. We got a couple of clouds to prove it."

"The p.m. showed poison, didn't it?"

"Yes. Morphine. In her condition, one grain was enough to finish her."

"Have you made any progress?"

"She died this morning, Smith, and we only got the jurisdiction question settled an hour ago and if you don't mind," he added with heavy sarcasm, "the department will tag along while you solve it. So start talking."

In a flat voice, Cellini recited: "I boarded one of the Continental Airlines planes that make the overnight jump from New York to L.A. with about a dozen other passengers. It was smooth sailing till Salt Lake. There the passenger agent told us that a storm was reported ahead and that the company would send us the rest of the way by train, if we wanted, but that there was no real danger. The Department of Commerce wasn't grounding the plane. Most of the passengers chose the train. Besides Bella Riddle and myself, only Tubby Moore, his wife and a drip-face called David H. Haring finished it by air. By the way, what have you learned about this Haring?"

"He's a junior partner in a New York investment house and he's opening a west coast branch for them."

"Is he known around here?"

"A little," said the Homicide man. "He's been flying back and forth the last few months. Have you a client on this case, Smith?"

"Yes."

"Tell me about Bella Riddle on the trip."

"Nothing special," replied Cellini. "She slept most of the way. There must have been something wrong with her because every once in a while she'd wake up and take a couple of small white pills from a phial. Did the medical examiner find out for what?"

THE HOMICIDE MAN nodded. "She had chronic nephritis." He consulted a card from his pocket. "To be exact, she had arteriosclerotic kidneys with an end result of pre-existing hypertension. My grandmother used to call it kidney trouble." He replaced the card. "Tell me, Smith, who's your client?"

"What kind of pills were they?" asked Cellini deliberately.

"Sodium nitrate. Who'd you say your client was, Smith?"

Cellini stared at him blankly.

"I see," said Haenigson. "The sanctity of the client and similar clatrap. You noticed nothing else on the trip?"

"Nothing."

"The plane hostess handed us a crossword puzzle book," Haenigson said. "In it you wrote that Bella Riddle was murdered. Why?"

"Well, the p.m. shows she died from morphine and I figured something like that had happened. She had been taking pills throughout the trip with no ill effect. Then suddenly, with no one noticing, she sank into a coma and died. I figured that somebody had switched pills on her."

"What made you figure that?"

"The whole phial of pills was spilled over her lap. She seemed to sense there was something wrong with them and, before she passed out, she probably started examining them. The pills were switched after we left Salt Lake—and that couldn't have been difficult because she slept most of the time."

The Homicide man nodded. "But who did the switching?"

"Anybody. The passengers all had to pass her to go to the can in the back. Have you been able to find out anything about this Bella Riddle yet?"

"Not much, Smith. It looks like she had no family. She was coming out here to live off her income."

Cellini produced the whiskey bottle and they each downed two fingers. Haenigson said: "I know that Pete showed you Bella Riddle's stuff. What'd you think?"

"Same as you. Who is Mr. Benson and why didn't he meet the plane?"

"Must be a friend of some friend and he just ducked. We'll find him."

"That remains to be seen," said Cellini cryptically.

Haenigson caught the odd inflection but didn't pursue the

point. Cellini remembered the hundred dollars in his pocket and the promise of another five hundred. He said: "Tubby Moore looks like the best candidate for the job."

Ira Haenigson shook his head.

"Why not? A racketeer like him—"

"I'll tell you" interposed the Homicide man. "Because Bella Riddle wasn't murdered. That's why not."

"What! Oh—so that's how it is. I didn't think Tubby was so important you'd be scared to tag him."

Haenigson's pancake face reddened. "See here, Smith—"

"Sure, sure," said Cellini. "I know. We've got the best police force that money can buy. But suppose you tell me why you think she wasn't murdered."

"Because those pills in her lap were legitimate and nobody switched them. They were sodium nitrate—not morphine."

"Then how come she died of morphine?"

"For all I know," said the detective-sergeant, "she was a drug addict and the morphine caught up with her at last. These scientific criminologists can sometimes be wrong. But it's more likely that a morphine tablet got mixed in with the sodium pills. Those accidents can happen. We're checking with Wood-row Pharmacists in New York. They made up the prescription."

Cellini frowned. It was difficult to see how the pills could have been switched back a second time after death. He said: "That would make things easy, wouldn't it? A friendless, old lady gets murdered and because you're lazy it becomes an accident."

Haenigson uttered something soft and monosyllabic and left.

Cellini Smith waited till he heard the outside door bang shut, then reached for the telephone book. He riffled the pages, found the number of the airline company and dialed. It was the police calling, he informed them. Was Miss Margery Lyons, hostess on Flight 6, still in the city? She was? Fine. There were a few points still to be cleared up on the Riddle case—discreetly, of course—so what was her address? Hotel Edwards? Many thanks...

Cellini cradled the receiver and locked the office. Haenigson's theory that the death was an accidental homicide might be his way of paying rope out to the suspects. Besides, the airline's operatives wouldn't throw in the towel so soon. But murder or not, Cellini decided the case had a piscatorial odor.

CELLINI SMITH HANDED the desk clerk at the Hotel Edwards an empty envelope and asked him to leave it in Miss Margery Lyons' box. He saw the envelope slipped into compartment 317. He lingered over some travel brochures till the desk clerk was occupied, then stepped into an elevator and rode up to the third floor.

He moved down the carpeted corridor till he found his number and knocked.

"Hello, you're early," called Margery Lyons as she opened the door.

Cellini never noticed the utter change in her expression. He was engrossed by the clinging beige gown that was in no way allergic to her figure. "Can I come in?" he finally remembered to ask.

"Yes, but only for a moment. I'm expecting somebody. A dinner engagement." She didn't invite him to sit down but stood in the center of the room, frowning, waiting for him to speak.

"Is that the boy-friend who likes your perfume?"

"Please, Mr. Smith, an air hostess' private life must have nothing to do with the passengers. If you have any reason for searching me out here, then please state it."

"I thought we were friends, Miss Lyons, and you double-crossed me by turning that crossword book over to the cops."

"I'm sorry but I had to. It was my duty."

"It's all right. Forget it."

"If that's all, Mr. Smith, I won't keep you."

Cellini sat into an easy chair and lit a cigarette. He watched the impatient tattoo of her open-toe slipper with some amusement. "Miss Lyons, there's something important I want you to try and remember. Give me the answer and I'll go before Lochinvar gets here," he said disarmingly.

"All right, Mr. Smith, but please ask it."

"Bella Riddle had to take pills at stated intervals on account of some kind of kidney trouble."

She nodded. "Yes, I remember her taking them."

"Well, some time after we left Salt Lake one of the passengers exchanged the pill bottle for one containing morphine tablets. That wasn't very difficult because it was in the early dawn and most of us passengers were exhausted and drowsy. But then, after she died, the pills were switched a second time. And that was almost difficult enough to be impossible. Do you remember anybody stopping by Mrs. Riddle's seat after she was dead?"

The impatient tapping ceased for a moment and her brow contracted. Cellini wondered if she had a boy friend in every airport. "No, I can't remember," was her considered reply.

"Think, Miss Lyons. Somebody stopping at that seat for

a few seconds—just long enough to scoop up the morphine tablets and phial and replace them with sodium nitrate."

"I'm sorry. If I remembered I'd tell you."

"Is the name Benson familiar to you?"

"No."

"All right, Miss Lyons. If anything occurs to you later, I'll be at home. The number is Hempstead 1919."

"Yes. Now if you'll leave—" Her phone sounded off.

Cellini didn't stir. "Answer it," he said. "It might be the boy-friend."

She flashed him a look that could have wilted an artificial flower and picked up the receiver. She spoke guardedly. "Hello... No, not right now... Someone's up here... In a little—"

"Just tell David Haring to come up," cut in Cellini.

Her hand went over the mouthpiece. "Mr. Smith! What makes you think that—"

"I'm a great detective, Miss Lyons. I know that Haring's in the lobby as sure as I know that you're not wearing a girdle. Ask the windbag to come up."

SHE SPOKE INTO the mouthpiece in a flat, apathetic voice. "Come up, Dave."

She let the receiver drop and when she turned, her face was pale and strained. "Mr. Smith, since you know so much, I might as well tell you that Dave Haring and I are engaged."

"Congratulations. I'll send you a sinister clue for a wedding present."

"That's not why I tell you. I want it kept a secret. I'd lose my job if the company discovered that I dated a passenger."

"I thought you were getting married."

"Yes, but it's not that simple. Dave has a wife in New York and they're arranging a divorce settlement now. That takes time. And if Mrs. Haring found out Dave and I were in love she'd make difficulties."

"O.K. It's no concern of mine—provided it has no bearing on Bella Riddle."

"It hasn't, Mr. Smith. And Dave has nothing to do with—"

The door opened and David H. Haring entered. An implausible diamond, sparkling in his tie, accentuated the air of phoney prosperity. An eyebrow raised at sight of Cellini but he took the situation in his stride. "Ha-ha, if it isn't Smith old boy trying to cut in on my little girl." He pumped Cellini's hand as if it were an ice cream freezer.

"How do you know my name?"

"Can't trip me on that one, old boy. Margery told me."

"He knows we're engaged," Miss Lyons interposed hurriedly.

"Swell," boomed the investment man too heartily. "I suppose you were trying to bully the little gal, Smithy, but she knows nothing of Mrs. Riddle's death. In fact, my little cherub told me the police decided it wasn't murder. Just a druggist's mistake. So why all the investigating if—"

Cellini raised a hand to stem the verbiage. "You ought to hire a room with an echo—hear yourself better. Just try to tell me in one word if you know Tubby Moore."

"Tubby Moore..." He scratched at his chin as he made an effort to remember.

"That short, fat guy in the plane," reminded Cellini.

"Oh, sure. A Casper Milquetoast kind of guy. Don't know him though. But why harp on these things, Smithy, if the police say the case is closed?"

"Perhaps," explained Cellini patiently, "the police are releasing phoney statements just to lull everybody's suspicions. Besides, the airline company has hired its own outfit of private dicks to investigate and I'll lay a corn-pad to that glass rock in your ascot that one of their shadows will tail you as you leave the hotel.

Margery Lyons and her fiancé exchanged glances. When Haring's laugh sounded it rang hollow.

"Ha-ha-ha, if they follow us they better have plenty of mazuma on them. We're going to the Cocoanut Grove and dinners are damned expensive there!"

5

Gunsel and Op

IN THE HOTEL lobby, Cellini sat waiting glumly. It was now a half hour since he had left windy Haring and his girl but they still hadn't come down. Maybe it was a mistake to tell them they'd be tailed. But what were they waiting for? Again Cellini looked at his watch. It was nearing seven and he was getting short on temper and long on hunger. He decided an olive might dull his appetite so he flagged a bellhop and asked him to fetch a martini from the bar.

The one consolation was that colorless man at the other end of the lobby, trying to read a newspaper upside down. It was the shadow from Munson's who had attached himself to Haring at the airport that morning. It was good to know there was someone else who hadn't had dinner. The little Burke was nowhere in evidence. Cellini wondered what he was up to. The shifty, little weasel…

The bellhop arrived with the cocktail. Cellini produced a dollar. "This is for your old age if you go up to room three seventeen and ask if they called for room service. Take a look inside and report back."

The boy palmed the bill and left. In two minutes he was back. "Nobody answered, mister."

"Nobody?"

"Yeah—nobody."

"Is there a side exit to this place?"

"Yup. Down the corridor there in the back."

Cellini swore. He had been a damned fool—a bush league operative. The only thing left was to see whether David Haring had lied—to check whether he and his fiancée were really at the Cocoanut Grove.

He turned on his heel and left.

CELLINI SMITH SCANNED the diners and dancers. No David Haring and no Margery Lyons. But then he hadn't really expected to find them. About to leave, he espied a familiar head of auburn hair.

Ginger Moore sat alone at a table for two, finishing dinner with a *demi-tasse*. He made a short end-run around the left side of a line of waiters and reached her table.

"May I sit down?"

She nodded and those thin hard lips relaxed to say: "Please do. I've been wondering how you were getting along."

"Me too," he said drily.

"You mean you're convinced of my husband's innocence?"

"Not yet, Mrs. Moore. You can still hope for a divorce via the electric chair."

"It's not a joking matter, Mr. Smith."

"I'll say it isn't. I never laugh at five hundred bucks. Tell me, Mrs. Moore, why you say you can't leave your husband when Tubby says you can go anytime you like."

"What difference does it make?"

"The difference is, Mrs. Moore, that I'd know whether or not I can trust you—whether you're dealing them straight or from behind a corkscrew."

"I bought your trust with a hundred dollars," she reminded him.

"Um." He smiled ruefully and wondered if she ate scrap iron for breakfast cereal. "I guess we can look at it that way, Mrs. Moore. How come you're dining alone?"

"My husband threw me out of our house for an hour or two."

"As bad as that?"

"Oh, Tubby was very polite about it," she said. "He quoted Shakespeare and said he expected guests and would I mind dining alone."

"What guests?"

"He didn't say, Mr. Smith, but I wish *you'd* say what you've accomplished."

"A single fact," said Cellini. "That Bella Riddle did not die accidentally. She was killed on a plane in the hope that death would be laid to heart failure—that murder would seem preposterous. If that went wrong, the murderer still hoped that death would be blamed on some negligent druggist who supplied the harmless sodium pills."

Ginger Moore asked more questions but Cellini suddenly began to feel hungry. He muttered something conventional and escaped.

Cellini Smith first stopped at his office. The long-distance operator had no call waiting but under the door was another wire from Sampsel. It conveyed the curious information that a few weeks ago Bella Riddle had surprised a thief in her bathroom. The thief escaped.

Some twenty minutes later, Cellini graced the counter of his favorite chophouse. He tried not to think of the rare filet being readied in the charcoal broiler and forced his thoughts to dwell on the case. The vaguest glimmer of an idea began shaping in his brain. It needed little, he felt—perhaps some stray item of information—to bring it into focus.

What, he asked himself again, had Tubby Moore, a washed-up racketeer, to do with David Haring and Haring with him? And both with Bella Riddle—an old woman coming to California to live off her income? Live off her income!

Abruptly the fragments of fact and surmise stopped whirling and fell into place. The relationship between Haring and the racketeer was suddenly plain. It was clear, too, why Ginger Moore was dining alone—and who were Tubby Moore's expected guests. And he knew how the morphine tablets had been switched back into pills of sodium nitrate.

The steak arrived. Cellini glared at it, grabbed a potato chip and his hat and lammed out. It was vital to reach Tubby Moore's apartment without delay.

THE TIRES OF Cellini's coupé screeched as he turned from Wilshire into Bedford and raced down the street. A few seconds later, he braked opposite Tubby Moore's apartment. All available parking space was taken so he cut the motor and double-parked. Time was important.

He crossed the street and gained the sidewalk as a man stepped from behind a car and blocked his path. A nearby street lamp lighted his face. It belonged to Tubby Moore's gorilla—Lou. The lips were puffed out and bluish and sufficiently parted to reveal three empty sockets that were recently hosts to as many yellowed teeth.

Lou nodded toward the service alley on the north side of the building. "Get—quick!"

Cellini complied, for in Lou's right hand was a flat .32 automatic persuader that pointed to the pit of his stomach. The service alley was narrow and dark—lighted only by the globe over the door at the far end. Garbage cans cluttered one side. A malevolent tomcat spat at them and padded into the darkness.

"I knew you'd come back, Smith. I knew damn well you'd come back." The missing teeth gave Lou's words a quaint hissing quality. But Cellini Smith wasn't inclined to laughter.

"You knew I'd come back where?" stalled Cellini.

"Right here, you smart dick. Right here where they're going to find you."

Cellini waited, his body tense—waited for the blue barrel of the pistol to waver, to relax for one brief instant. But it didn't. "I beat up on you," he said, "and you come back with a gat. Brave boy."

"You ——! You know it ain't because you beat up on me."

"No? Then why am I getting it?"

The hood stiffened as a dark coupé pulled up across the street behind Cellini's car. Its license plate bore the boxed *E* of a departmental prowl car.

"One peep out of you," whispered Lou, "and you're a dead gilley."

There was a quality of desperation about Lou that made Cellini believe him. The gunsel knew his way around—probably had a get-away car beyond the alley. If only there was some way of attracting the attention of the shams!

A cop stepped out of the prowl car, strode over to the double-parked Plymouth and examined the registration card on the steering post. He produced a pad, put one foot on the running-board and began writing out a summons.

Cellini started to edge toward the garbage cans. He might be able to tip one over. The .32 jabbed into his stomach and scotched that.

The cop finished the leisurely writing of the ticket and left it on the steering wheel. He rejoined his partner and the prowl car moved off—taking Cellini's hopes with it.

"That just give you an extra two minutes to live," lisped Lou. Cellini's mind spun desperately. "You didn't tell me," he said. "What?"

"The reason for this."

"You're getting it because you gave it to him. That's why."

There was the clatter of feet on pavement and the silencing barrel of Lou's gun again prodded the pit of Cellini's stomach. Then Cellini's shadow—the little Burke—hove into view, crossing from the other side of the street. Could he attract his attention? Would the op notice them? But the little Burke passed by, a scant fifteen feet away, and turned into the apartment building.

CELLINI KNEW HE ought to keep talking. His mind revolved a dozen futile plans. "Listen, Lou, you're making a big mistake. If the cops find me here they'll go through the apartments and connect me with Tubby Moore. They'll hang it on Tubby, Lou. On your own boss."

"Hang it on Tubby?" Lou gave a barking laugh.

Suddenly every muscle in Cellini's body drew taut. The service door began inching open. Cellini edged sideways, compelling the gorilla to turn his back on the door. "Sure, Lou. That's who they'll pin it on." The ghost-like figure stepped from the service door into the alley.

"There's no worry about Tubby," said Lou harshly. "And don't think you can stall me, Smith, because you're through."

The figure was bearing down on Lou. Cellini could feel the

beads of sweat on his forehead. "I mean it, Lou. The shams'll pick you up before morning."

The noiseless figure glided within a yard of them.

The hood took a step forward. "You do your gabbing in hell, Smith, because you're on your way now!"

An arm shot up behind Lou and smashed down viciously. The gunsel crumpled into an inert heap with a whistling of air between the empty sockets.

Cellini Smith mopped his forehead with a handkerchief. The little Burke stood over the prostrate form and gazed at the sap in his hand with something akin to awe.

"I thought you'd never get to him," said Cellini.

"You were certainly right, Smith," declared the small operative. "A sap can make up for four inches any day."

"You're not as dumb as you look, Burke. You spotted us as you passed the alley, didn't you?"

"Uh-huh. I'm the little man who was really there." He still stared lovingly at the sap. "Now if I could only find some solution for the dames. They don't like little guys."

"Tell them," counseled Cellini absently, "that it's better to have loved a short man than never to have loved a-tall." He tried to think—guess what had happened. He knew he should hurry up to Tubby Moore's but he couldn't drag himself away from the alley. Something had gone wrong—something that had sent Lou gunning for him. He had to know what that was before doing anything else. He poked the unconscious gorilla with the toe of his foot. "Burke, do you know why he was gunning for me?"

"What did you expect him to do—kiss you?"

"Something happened, Burke. Something that made him want to get me pretty badly.

"What's on your mind, Smith? I saved your life so I got a right to know. I have a stake in you."

"Stake," growled Cellini. "Damn it, don't use that word."

"Come on. Talk."

"I'm not sure," frowned Cellini, "but Lou said he was giving it to me because I gave it to someone else. Why? And for that matter, Burke, what were *you* doing here?"

Burke snapped his fingers. "It's good you remind me. I nearly forgot." He reached down and picked up the .32 that had slipped from Lou's fingers. "I tried to stop you at your office, Smith, but you drove off too fast for me. You came in this direction so I took a chance and hopped a cab."

"What did you want?"

The little man leveled the automatic at Cellini's chest. "Cellini Smith," he said bombastically, "I hereby arrest you for the murder of Mrs. Bella Riddle."

CELLINI SIGHED. IF he hadn't been so hungry, he could have had a good laugh. "Burke," he said, "I hereby change my mind. On second thought, you *are* as dumb as you look."

"You almost got away with it," spoke Burke from his eminence of five feet two inches.

"Almost," agreed Cellini.

"You switched those pills, Smith, and I got proof you did."

"I forgot," said Cellini. "Why did I switch them?"

"You forget, do you?" Burke waved the pistol in his hand with wild carelessness. Cellini thought of stepping in and taking it away but decided to hear him out first.

"Exactly why you switched them, Smith, I don't know yet. But our New York office is working on that. You probably did some kind of dirty work, pulled some kind of frame on a friend of Bella Riddle's. She was probably coming out here to find you and turn you over to the cops. That's why you went to New York—to get her before she could show you up."

"You have found me out, you monster," said Cellini. "And what mysterious clue did I leave lying around for you to discover?"

Burke's left hand dug into his jacket pocket and came up with a small phial. It was a duplicate of the one Cellini had seen in the lap of the dead Bella Riddle that morning. "You thought you were smart," crowed Burke. "You thought if I searched your office once, I wouldn't do it again. You thought—"

"Shut up, Burke! Are there morphine tablets in that?"

Burke took a tighter grip on the pistol and stepped a little closer. "You know it's morphine, Smith—and don't think you can take it away from me."

"What made you think of looking in my office again?"

"About an hour ago, somebody phoned our agency and tipped us off."

"Was it a man or a woman, Burke?"

"A woman, but what difference does it make? The point is, I got the goods on you. I don't know where Tubby Moore fits in yet, but I'll find that out too. Maybe he sent his hood gunning for you because you tried to blackmail Tubby or something."

"Blackmail!" At last it was clear to Cellini what Lou had meant. It was more than revenge for the loss of a few teeth. "Pack the gun," he said. "I've got to get out of here."

Burke laughed and moved in closer. A newsboy on a bicycle pedaled by and braked short to stare into the alley with pop-eyes. "Hey, kid," called Burke. "I'm a detective. Go to the drugstore on the corner and phone for the cops."

The boy was off like a bat out of hell. Cellini started to leave.

"Don't move," said Burke. "You had to teach me what good a sap was but you can't tell me anything about this height-equalizer in my hand. You're gonna wait till the shams get here."

"You're just a half-baked amateur," said Cellini impatiently. He indicated the figure of the gorilla. "Lou, at least, knew his business—you don't."

"Do tell," taunted the little Burke.

"Sure. In the first place, Burke, you're too close to me. Second, you're dumb enough to point the gun at my heart instead of my belly because you got a romantic notion that a guy falls quicker with a slug in his heart than in his stomach. You don't realize that I just have to shift right—"

Cellini suited action to the word. Burke's gun-arm came around and Cellini's left hand shot up, caught it and twisted backward. The pistol clattered to the sidewalk as Burke was forced to his knees and Cellini reached down and pocketed the weapon.

Burke stood up, trembling, his face drained of blood. Cellini unknotted his necktie. "Lie down on your stomach," he said. "Hurry up before I bounce you around like a pogo stick!"

The small operative did as he was bid and Cellini tied his wrists firmly together behind his back. He next slipped his own tie off and lashed Burke's ankles together. Then Cellini dragged him to one side and wedged him between two garbage cans filled with ashes.

"That'll hold you," he said, "and you better not do any yelling. When the cops get here, tell them I went up to Tubby Moore's to look for a dead body."

6

Dividends

THE DOOR TO Tubby Moore's apartment was ajar. Cellini Smith pushed it open and entered. The racketeer lay sprawled over the rug. He had quoted Shakespeare for the last time.

While never a pretty sight in life, Tubby Moore was even less so in death. His blood-caked head was bashed in—evidently by the lead paperweight that was ludicrously perched on his conspicuous stomach. His right hand, Napoleon-like, was inside his jacket, still reaching for a gun, and the other pudgy hand still clawed at the thick throat as it had at the moment that death had overtaken him.

"Hello! Let's drink a toast to Tubby's murder. Like he'd say, 'It's a knell that summoned him to heaven or to hell.'"

It was Ginger Moore speaking. She sat on a couch, glass in hand, fifth of Scotch at her side, and drunk to the ears. The auburn hair was disheveled and her gown stained with spilled liquor.

"What happened?" Cellini asked.

She giggled inanely. "What, no toast? Well I like you anyway, Mr. Smith. You're no Robert Taylor but you have points."

"What happened?"

She waved toward the body, sending a spray of Scotch over the rug. "That. Tubby's organizing a lottery in hell right this minute."

"Was he dead when you got back from the Cocoanut Grove?"

"My own little, darling Tubby. Dead from lead on the head."
She giggled again and downed some Scotch.

He walked over and shook her shoulders. "Snap out of it.
What happened when you got here?"

"Be nice, Mr. Smith. Nice like a lice on some ice, or I won't
let you spend Tubby's money with me."

Cellini said harshly: "I wouldn't touch you with a pair of
forceps, sister. I want information."

She drew back and leered at him with clouded eyes. "You
wouldn't? I gave you a hundred dollars and now you're mad
because you can't get the other five hundred. Because you can't
prove my blubbery Tubby killed that woman. You can't, you
can't."

"I can't because he didn't do it. Did you see anyone when you
got back here?"

"I saw Tubby, that's who." She hiccuped and drank again.
"Drink a toast to my hubby, Tubby. He's being toasted two
ways now."

"Listen and stop that drinking. You got back here and Tubby
was dead. Then Lou showed up and the gorilla thought I did
it and went gunning for me. That's what happened, isn't it?"

"A toast to a ghost who'll roast," she mumbled.

"For God's sake, snap out of it. Did you touch anything
on the body? Did you find anything—see anybody? Try to
remember. It's important."

"Heaven or hell," she said thickly.

"Listen, the cops'll be here right away and I want you to tell
them I've gone to the Hotel Edwards and—"

Without warning, Ginger Moore went limp and sank back
on the couch and the glass slipped from her fingers. The hard

face seemed to relax into some blissful dream of dozens of murdered Tubby Moores.

"Come on," urged Cellini. "Pull yourself together." He grabbed her by the shoulder, yanked her into a sitting posture and began slapping her face back and forth. But the body remained limp and the glazed eyes showed no signs of returning consciousness. He swore and let her go.

He scanned the room for a moment and finally found pencil and paper in a secretary. He hastily wrote a note saying he'd gone to the Hotel Edwards and dropped it near the body. The late Tubby Moore's wife started to snore gently.

Cellini dashed out and down the stairs. He could hear, in the distance, the approaching sirens of the police cars.

AS CELLINI SMITH strode down the corridor of the Hotel Edwards for the second time that day, he paused to pull in his belt two more notches. The way he felt he would have wolfed a thirty-five-cent vegetable plate.

He knocked on the door of room 317.

Margery Lyons' voice called, "It's open," and Cellini walked in.

David H. Haring and the air hostess were seated at a service table drinking brandied coffees. The table was littered with silver and napery, as if they had just completed a meal. Cellini grabbed at a crust of bread and sat down between them.

"We thought you were the waiter, Smithy," came Haring's booming voice. "Ha-ha, at that, you're always waiting for us."

"You've been here all the time?" asked Cellini.

"That's right."

"I thought you were taking Miss Lyons to the Cocoanut Grove."

"Changed my mind. Decided to eat here. You scared the pants off me, Smithy, when you said we'd be followed."

"That was about three hours ago. How's it you're only finishing your dinner now?"

"Margery and I were talking things over and, you rascal, don't ask what we were talking about."

"How come that a half-hour after I left, a bellhop couldn't find anyone in here?"

"Damn it, Smith!" exclaimed Haring. "Did you send that bellhop around? Marge and I were staring out at the moon and we didn't feel like answering any knock on the door just then. Ha-ha, neither would you."

"You can't see the moon from that window."

Haring turned swiftly and gazed out. "Look," he said with some relief. "It's right there."

Cellini laughed.

"Mr. Smith," said Margery Lyons in a strained voice, "Dave was here all the time. Why don't you believe him?"

"Because I know he wasn't. He was keeping an appointment with Tubby Moore."

"Ha-ha-ha."

"And they had a fight and he pushed in Tubby's skull with a lead paperweight. With his wonderful sense of humor, he left the weight on top of Tubby's belly and came back here. Then Ginger Moore went home, saw her husband dead and got drunk to celebrate. Later, one of Tubby's hoods arrived, figured I'd done the job and went gunning for me."

Haring bellowed again. "Smithy, you can dream 'em up better than Dali. But why should I even want to see that Tubby Moore? That's one for *Information, Please*, ha-ha-ha."

"Tubby was cutting in on your organization, Haring. He was washed-up here, but he still had good connections in the underworld and he heard of your outfit. He went to New York just to check on it. Maybe someone right in your outfit was tipping him off to the whole racket. Tubby heard you were coming out here to open a branch and he trailed you. At Salt Lake he changed his mind only because he was following you and you were following Bella Riddle."

"Smithy," chortled Haring, "you're wonderful. When my cherub and I have a kid, we'll get you to tell it bedtime stories."

THE DOOR WAS thrust wide and Detective-sergeant Ira Haenigson, the little Burke and a couple of department men strode in. The tendons in the Homicide man's neck stood out in angry welts. "Smith," he demanded, "what's this run-around you're giving us? What happened to Tubby Moore? Who killed him?"

Cellini jerked a finger at David Haring. "That's your baby. You should have figured it yourself, when you found out that Bella Riddle was coming out here to live off her income. Is that income in the form of stocks and bonds?"

The Homicide man nodded, the little Burke's eyes went wide with interest, and Margery Lyons gave a queer, choked gasp.

"Then I'm right," continued Cellini. "David Haring is a member of a phoney investment house—a big-time bucket shop. What they do is look for people like Bella Riddle with no family and bad health. These Bella Riddles invest their dough with them and they make the first ten or fifteen dividend payments promptly. Then—"

"What about this man Benson who was supposed to meet Bella Riddle?" interrupted Haenigson.

"You'll never find him," said Cellini, "because there is no Benson. If you remember, the note says *our* Mr. Benson. So it was a business firm that wrote it. It was a business firm that bought the ticket and that knew Bella Riddle would be dead when she got here. Haring followed her to see it happened. This is a new wrinkle on a murder syndicate, Haenigson. Make phoney investments for sick and friendless clients and then arrange natural deaths. Tubby Moore heard of it, and he was trying to blackmail his way into the west coast branch that Haring was setting up here."

"Excuse me," put in Haring, "but do you remember me? The guy you're trying to frame? I want to know how you expect to prove any of this."

"Have you been able to find out who invested Bella Riddle's money for her?" Cellini asked the Homicide man.

"An outfit called Eastern States Investment."

"Good," said Cellini. "O.K., Haring, have you anything to do with that outfit? We'll find out easy enough, so you might as well tell us."

"I'm telling you nothing, Smith. I want a lawyer."

"You'd need a Houdini to get you out of it," replied Cellini. "Your murder syndicate never thought that anybody would figure Bella Riddle could be murdered on a plane. They thought it would be blamed on heart failure, and that if it came to a p.m., the druggists would be blamed for accidentally slipping a morphine pill in with the others. You've got a very careful outfit, Haring. A few weeks ago, one of your men was almost caught searching the bathroom of Bella Riddle's home. That man was trying to find out where Bella Riddle got her prescriptions filled."

"Look, Smith," said Haenigson, "I can see how this egg could have killed Moore but how did he get at the Riddle dame without anyone seeing him?"

"Yeah," cut in Burke, "and what about those morphine tablets in your office?"

"I'm coming to it," replied Cellini. "I know that Tubby Moore told his wife that he was expecting *guests* tonight and not *a* guest. So the one besides Haring was Margery Lyons—the murderer of Bella Riddle."

The hostess stared at him with wide, frightened eyes.

"Those morphine pills," continued Cellini, "were planted in my office and the only person who knew I wouldn't be there was Margery Lyons because I told her I was going home. Besides, it was a woman's voice, Burke, that tipped you people off to search my office again. Haring's been flying back and forth and he got acquainted with her and she joined their syndicate. Don't forget that the syndicate bought Bella Riddle her ticket, to make sure she'd be on Margery Lyons' plane. Who better to switch the sodium nitrate pills for morphine tablets? And finally, the big thing worrying me was how the morphine was switched a second time for the harmless nitrate pills when I was sitting awake right across the aisle. *Margery Lyons did it when she adjusted the safety belt on Bella Riddle!*"

Margery Lyons began to sob bitterly. "Shut up," said Haring out of the side of his mouth. "Just yell for a mouthpiece."

Cellini found a crumb on the tablecloth and surreptitiously swallowed it, as David Haring and Margery Lyons were led off. He noted a few drops remaining in the brandy glass and gulped them down.

Ira Haenigson sighed and patted his midriff. "All this excitement," he pronounced, "and all this running around is very bad on a full stomach—so soon after dinner."

Detective-sergeant Haenigson could never figure out why Cellini Smith hurled that brandy glass at him.

The Cat With a Headache

*"Is it fair if I use both hands?" was all Cellini
Smith wanted to know when young Mr. Forrest
handed him that half-grand sheaf of lettuce
as a come-on fee to undertake the cure of his
favorite feline's migraine. Little did L.A.'s
toughest private peep know that lead pellets
from a blue-steel bottle instead of the usual
mono-acetic-acidester-of-salicylic-acid tablets
would be needed to bring relief to the patient.*

1

Cat's-paw

CARL FORREST WAS young and handsome but he had the bloodshot eyes and faintly trembling fingers of the alcoholic, the loose skin and already-pouched neck of the unhealthy and the thin lips and razor-edge nose of the foul-tempered. All that Cellini Smith noted. But none of it interested him as much as the five hundred dollars bunched in Forrest's hands.

Cellini Smith said: "Let's not kid each other, mister. People don't come in here and pass out all that wampum just because they like my perfume."

"Of course, I expect you to do something for it," replied Carl Forrest.

"Sure, but the first thing you do is signal with that cabbage to make me take your proposition. Whatever the job is, I know I'd be a sucker to touch it. Besides, why come to me? I'm pretty new in this town but there are plenty of other dicks."

"I heard you were tough."

Cellini Smith leaned back in the swivel chair and looked into the rheumy eyes across the desk. "I knew it was a phoney proposition. Let's have it."

"Do you know of a gin-mill called the Black Cat?"

"In the Valley on Ventura Boulevard?" asked Cellini. "Paint remover for bar Scotch?"

"That's it. Only I never had the bravery to taste their bar Scotch. Anyway, your job is to get them out of there."

"That should be easy," said Cellini. "Is it fair if I use both hands?"

"I don't care how you do it but I want you to make them break the lease and move out of there. I'll give you this five hundred dollar retainer and another five hundred if you succeed in moving them out."

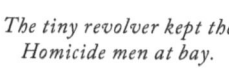

The tiny revolver kept the Homicide men at bay.

"That's a lot of money."

Carl Forrest shrugged impatiently. "It's a lot of work."

"Let's see how it goes. You want me to walk into the Black Cat and tell them to pack their duffle and move to another location. Right?"

"Yes."

"And what if they tell me to go up a creek and they call the cops? And what if the cops listen to the story and take my license away and put me in mothballs for the winter?"

Forrest hooked one of Cellini's cigarettes from a package on the desk and lit it. "They won't call the cops. They might beat

up on you and they might even kill you. That'll be your worry. But they won't call the cops."

"That's comforting. Why not?"

"Because they have a gambling layout in the back. Roulette, dice and Canfield."

"Ah." Cellini Smith flashed the twisted, friendly smile that was characteristic of him but the rest of the strong-boned face was unsmiling. He propped his feet on an open desk drawer and the lean tapered body tilted still further back in the swivel chair. "Who runs the joint?"

"Did you ever hear of the Cobra?" countered Carl Forrest. Cellini nodded.

"Then you know what you're up against. The Cobra owns it and she has a sort of general manager called Lee Boyce. He's a gambler from St. Louis and he seems to be her current boy friend."

Cellini shook his head thoughtfully. "Something stinks. I still don't see why they couldn't call the shams if I invited them to pretty please get out of there. They wouldn't even be operating if they weren't paying out protection."

"Sure they're paying protection. But it's to be let alone—not to be protected."

"I guess so," admitted Cellini.

"Besides, if it's your license that worries you, forget it. If you have it revoked my uncle is important enough to get it back for you."

"What is he—a printer?"

"My uncle," said Carl Forrest with an impressive pause, "is Abner Truman."

Cellini Smith allowed himself a long, low whistle. Abner

Truman was a household name. The man was discouragingly wealthy, with vast real estate holdings and oil properties, and a professional philanthropist and head of many charities.

Cellini said: "I'm beginning to get it. Your uncle owns the Black Cat property and, being a pillar of the church, he's afraid the liquor and gambling might give him a bad name. So I'm supposed to be his Carrie Nation and get them out of there."

"The details are colored," replied Forrest, "but the general outline is quite correct."

Cellini Smith stood up. He was two inches shy of six feet but the limbs were long and the body had a supple, athletic grace. He said: "Let's go visit Uncle Abner."

"What for? I've told you all that's necessary."

"I don't trust you."

"I assure you I'm authorized to act for Mr. Truman. In fact, this money belongs to him."

"That's just why I want to see him. Let's go."

FOLLOWING CARL FORREST'S directions, Cellini Smith turned into Coldwater Canyon Road and they began to climb the steep grade winding up into the hills.

Five minutes later they reached a large wooded estate. A gardener, working a gasoline-powered lawn mower, opened the gate and they sped up the driveway. Doors opened, flunkies announced, indirect lighting came on and in less time than it takes to say "tax exempt government bonds" Cellini Smith found himself sitting in the library opposite Abner Truman. He divided his attention between his host and the glass of fine brandy in his hand.

Abner Truman was tall and spare with slate-gray hair and the frank, open face of one who was too wealthy to bother about being dishonest. He was saying: "All my nephew has told you is quite correct, Mr. Smith. I left the size of your fee to his own discretion and I think the assignment is sufficiently dangerous to offer you a thousand dollar retainer instead of five hundred and another thousand if you succeed."

Cellini regretfully allowed the last drop of brandy to trickle down his throat. "I'd like to speak to you privately," he said.

Abner Truman nodded to his nephew. Carl Forrest emitted an angry grunt and stamped from the room.

Cellini reached for the brandy bottle again. "There's something I can't put my finger on, Mr. Truman. In the first place, why do you want the Black Cat dispossessed?"

"They're a little too notorious. Everyone knows I own that property and it hurts my standing in the community. That gambling establishment is a thorn in my side. I'm not one of these moralists who is a great reformer in the church but who rents houses to bordellos on the side."

"How did they get a lease in the first place?"

"My nephew takes care of those things and he rented it to what he thought would be a restaurant because I don't even allow bars on my places. Then it turned out to be not only a bar but a gambling establishment. Unfortunately, Carl didn't have enough sense to stipulate, in the lease, exactly what kind of business it would have to be."

A young girl glided into the room and, without seeming to notice Cellini, walked up to Abner Truman. Her girdleless figure, Cellini decided, was something to write home about in a special delivery letter. The profile and the side of the face he could see was delicate, sensitive and peculiarly sad under flowing auburn curls.

Tunelessly, she said: "I want more money. Let me have a blank check."

"Yes, my dear." The elderly Abner Truman's voice was mild. He reached for pen and check book in his pocket. "Excuse me. Mr. Smith, my niece—Loraine Forrest."

Cellini mumbled an acknowledgment. She turned toward him and he was now able to see the other side of her face. It bore a scar—a wide, permanent gash that extended from her temple almost to her cleft chin.

She touched her cheek. "Very bad, isn't it, Mr. Smith?"

"It's certainly not good, Miss Forrest."

She nodded a wordless agreement, pulled the signed check from her uncle's hand and walked out.

"Loraine is Carl's sister," said Abner Truman. "Their parents are both dead and I'm taking care of them. She got that mark on her face a few months ago in an automobile crash and she hasn't been herself since." His voice became bitter. "Shatter-proof glass! She was engaged but broke it off after it happened."

"She'll get over it after a while," remarked Cellini for want of better.

"Not her. The terrible thing is she blames me for the accident. I bought her a roadster and two months later she changed her mind and asked for a steelbody coupé. I put my foot down on such extravagance and now she claims that if I would have gotten her the closed coupé it wouldn't have happened." He fell silent.

After a while, Cellini said: "To get back to the point, Mr. Truman, how come you picked on me for this job?"

"I left that to my nephew Carl," the old man replied. "I told him to get a small agency and one with a reputation for toughness."

"Why a small one?"

"Because a big agency would involve too many people and my name must be kept out of it. You do your job, Mr. Smith, but if you slip, you're on your own. I won't recognize you."

"There's one more thing," said Cellini. "You're a pretty important man and while I know that the Black Cat pays protection, still you could raise hell and force the police to close them."

"I went to the police, Mr. Smith. They told me frankly that if I insisted they'd close the place but wouldn't accept the responsibility for my life. Those gamblers have a curious sense of honor. They have a lease and they pay the rent on time each month and they feel they have a right to stay there. They also have a heavy investment in the place and they've built up quite a trade—and the police have told me that they might consider it a breach of faith and try to kill me if I forced them out. Of course, I'd like to live as long as possible. That's why, whatever you do, my name must be kept out of it."

Cellini Smith said: "Let's have the thousand bucks."

THE BLACK CAT bounded over the neon sign after some invisible mouse. It was a quarter after six in the evening and it had just been switched into activity.

Cellini Smith tooled past the road-house and its parking lot and then pulled to the curb and turned off the motor. He walked back, pushed by the glazed-glass doors and entered.

A solitary customer graced the semicircular bar—a mild inoffensive-looking man drinking a beer. Cellini straddled a stool and called for a beer.

"Light or dark?" asked the bartender. He was large and angular with a hod carrier's neck and sloping shoulders and his teeth were prominent and yellow.

"Listen, buckteeth," said Cellini, "when you speak to me, say 'sir.'"

The bartender's abundant eyebrows drew together as he measured Cellini. He didn't seem to like what he saw for he drew a beer and set it on the bar. Scenting something interesting, the mild customer moved two stools closer.

"That'll be a dime," said the bartender.

"What time do the games start?" asked Cellini.

"Games?"

"You know. Ring around a posie with a magnetized roulette wheel."

"Your nose is running, mister. Pay that dime and go out and chase it."

Cellini wagged a finger. "Temper, temper." He took a mouthful of the beer and spat it in a wide arc across the bar. "It stinks," he commented.

"Is the beer really so bad?" asked the mild man. "I got a polyp in my nose and it ruins my sense of taste."

The bartender slowly wiped the few drops that had sprayed his face, then, with equal deliberation, his hand wrapped around a bottle.

"Think twice before you try it," said Cellini. "I got two howitzers and a Molotov bread-basket in my pockets."

"A dick. That's what you smell like." The bartender's voice was charged with suppressed fury.

Cellini put a finger to his lips. "I'm a well known G-man on a highly secret mission."

"G-man!" The bartender snorted derisively. "Yeah—G for garbage." He pressed hard on a buzzer set into the backbar.

"Are you really a G-man?" asked the mild customer.

Cellini shook his head sadly. "They flunked me out on account of etiquette."

At the far end of the bar, a curtained entrance parted and a tall woman, followed by a somewhat shorter male, came through. Though he had never seen her, Cellini knew that here was the Cobra.

The mild man delivered a lingering sigh. "She's sure built for a hayride," he whispered with awe.

The dark Latin beauty wore a vermilion gown and a leopard-skin jacket over her indiscreetly curved figure. Lips, fingernails, toenails that showed from the stockingless feet and the heavy ear pendants all were of a dark red hue. Her long hair was glossy black and abundant and kept in place with ornamental hair pins. Cellini had heard rumors about those heavy hair pins that struck quicker than the fangs of an adder.

He guessed that the dapper man next to her, with the blue serge suit and oily handsomeness, was Lee Boyce, the gambler. A killer from inclination rather than necessity.

"What's wrong?" The Cobra's voice had a throaty quality.

"This baby's nosing around and getting a little too tough," supplied the bartender.

"What you want to do that for?" asked Lee Boyce.

"I'm an imp," said Cellini. "Me and Mickey Rooney."

"He's heeled," the bartender cautioned.

"That's right, buckteeth," nodded Cellini pleasantly. "What's more, I can shoot the tail-light off a firefly on a moonless night."

LEE BOYCE STUCK two well-groomed fingers into his mouth and emitted a shrill whistle. In a moment, somebody built like a rhinoceros and wearing tweeds you could hear from afar, lumbered through the curtained entrance from the rear.

The mild man dropped some change on the counter, mumbled, "I got an appointment," and pulled a fast fade.

"Stick around, Hannibal," said Lee Boyce to the rhino. "This guy's feeling his oats."

Hannibal grunted and came for Cellini Smith. He moved slowly but as inevitably as a ten ton truck. Cellini gauged the timing to a nicety. He braced himself against the bar and waited till the gorilla was almost on top of him. Then his foot lashed out viciously and caught Hannibal in the pit of his stomach.

The gorilla emitted a single, high moan of pain and rolled over backwards twice. He lay still for a few moments, panting heavily. Suddenly he leaped up—to freeze when he saw a blunt, pocket Colt in Cellini's hand.

"That's smart, Hannibal." Cellini backed away the better to cover them all.

Lee Boyce began inching forward when the Cobra put a restraining hand on his arm. She said to Cellini: "I can't guess who you are or what this is about but do you know who *we* are?"

"Sure," replied Cellini. "That's why I got this heater in my mitt. You're the Cobra and the boy friend is the undertaker's pal."

"What do you want?"

"I want you to pack up and get out of here. Move next door, across the street—any place. But get out of here."

"We pay out and we have a right to be here."

"I'm not interested in that. I just want you to move to another location."

"Beat it," said Lee Boyce. "You don't know what you're getting into. You'll be sorry you were ever born."

"What'll you do?" asked Cellini. "With the layout you got in the back room you can't send for the cops and I'll take my chance on Hannibal and the other hoods you got around here."

"It's a deal," murmured Lee Boyce. His eyes were almost closed and there was a faint smile on his lips.

The Cobra spoke. "Don't start your tricks again, Lee. You've made enough trouble for me already."

"This is one time there's gonna be a little more trouble."

She tapped him on the shoulder with long fingernails. "You always forget I'm the boss, Lee."

The gambler smiled mockingly. He was probably one of the few men not afraid of the Cobra.

She turned to Cellini. "I still don't understand you. What gives you the idea to try and get us out of here?"

"It makes no difference," Cellini replied. "I think there's oil under this building—that's probably where Lee Boyce gets the stuff for his hair—or maybe I just don't like the decorations."

As if to emphasize his words, Cellini picked up the beer glass with his free hand and sent it hurtling against the opposite wall. It shattered over a pink maiden who was coyly bathing in a fountain. Beyond a muttered oath from the bartender, none of the four reacted.

The Cobra said: "You're either a detective or crazy—or both. Who are you working for?"

"A fumigation service," stated Cellini. He began to back out. "I just wanted us to meet. We'll see more of each other later and maybe this'll ripen into a deep and lasting friendship."

He reached the glazed-glass swinging doors, his arm brought

the automatic around twice and two panes of glass shattered to the floor. He said, "Count ten before you think of chasing out after me," then disappeared.

2

—

Spinning Wheels

FOR TWO HOURS Cellini Smith checked on Lee Boyce and the Cobra. The unanimous opinion was that they were very nice people to stay away from.

But thousand-dollar retainers don't grow on ketchup trees and Cellini retired to a restaurant to plan his next move. He topped a beef tartar with whiskey and black coffee, then found a phone booth. He dialed the Black Cat.

"Hello. I want to speak to the Cobra."

"You got the wrong number," replied a guttural voice.

"Bully for you. Now suppose you go and tell the Cobra that Cellini Smith wants to talk to her."

A silence, and several minutes later he heard the throaty voice. "You're a brave man, Mr. Smith—and a stupid one because if you had any brains you'd be out of the state by now."

"Save it," said Cellini. "If you want the answers to some of those questions you asked me this afternoon I'll give you the chance."

"I'd like that very much." There was something chilling in the voice.

"Fine," replied Cellini. "I'm in town, so if you want to, you can come and meet me right now."

"Where?"

"Neutral territory, Cobra. How about the drugstore at Hollywood and Vine?"

"In a half hour." The phone clicked off.

Cellini Smith cut through Laurel Canyon for the Valley. He pushed the ancient coupé to its limit and in less than fifteen minutes pulled up near the Black Cat. He declutched and stepped out of the car, leaving the motor idle.

It was already after ten and customers lined the bar three deep. Buckteeth had two assistants to help make up the drinks. Cellini couldn't blame Lee Boyce and the Cobra for wanting to hold on to this place.

New panes of glazed glass had been set into the doors. Cellini kicked backwards and shattered one of the panes. There was silence for only an instant. Drunks often did peculiar things.

Cellini walked toward the archway in the rear. Out of the corner of his eye he could see Buckteeth pressing away on the buzzer. Cellini reached the velour drapes without hindrance when suddenly they parted and he was confronted by Lee Boyce. Behind the gambler, loomed the mastodon figure of Hannibal.

Lee Boyce gave an exaggerated bow of welcome. "Come in."

Cellini passed into the inner room. It was large and modernistic with lots of angular chairs, lamps, and ashtrays that looked like something else. The games were getting a big play from men in tails and dinner jackets and women in gowns that belonged on burlesque runways.

Hannibal stood close to Cellini. His hands were in his pockets. Lee Boyce said: "It's a good business you're trying to cut in on."

"What am I trying to do?" asked Cellini.

"Cut in. Don't think I wasn't able to figure out your racket. You think that with a little slick muscle work you can scare us out of here and take over the place yourself."

"That's not a bad idea," said Cellini. "Maybe I'll let you work for me when I take over. You can be manager of the towels and pick up tips in the wash room."

LEE BOYCE'S DELICATE fingers flipped a straw-tipped cigarette into his mouth. He relished the conversation. "And how do you plan taking the place over?"

"I haven't decided yet. Maybe I'll hide three or four leprosy germs under the flooring or scatter tacks on the parking lot. But I guess it would be easier if I used Hannibal for a stink bomb."

"Now that you mention the parking lot," said Lee Boyce, "you can get to it through that door on the right. Start walking—quietly and slowly."

"No, thanks," said Cellini. "And don't try to shove because I'll scream 'mercy' right out loud before all these people."

Lee Boyce chuckled audibly. "So that's the idea! You think you can come here and bang the place up and we'll do nothing because there's a lot of customers around." His voice hardened. "Now start moving for that door. The first phoney sound out of you and Hannibal plays his sap on your skull. All we got to say is you're a tough drunk and nobody will think twice of it."

Hannibal moved a little closer.

Cellini didn't budge. "You're supposed to be a smart man, Boyce, but I guess it's a fake reputation."

"What are you getting at?" asked the gambler suspiciously.

"You actually think I'd walk into this cage without protecting myself! Let me ask you this: just how crazy are you about the Cobra?"

For once Lee Boyce seemed uncertain about what to say. He waited for Cellini to continue, his eyelids flickering and his face muscles tightening.

"You guessed it," said Cellini. "The Cobra left a little while ago to meet me in Hollywood and, as you see, she won't find me."

Lee Boyce seemed to regain his assurance. "She'll find you— in fact, she'll decide what to do with you when she gets back. Start moving for that door."

Cellini turned slightly to keep an eye on Hannibal and wagged a finger at the gambler. "You still don't get the idea. The Cobra isn't coming back here unless I leave hale and hearty. I had a couple of friends meet her and they're going to hold on to that nasty gleam in her eye until I get back on two feet and give the word."

Lee Boyce's sallow complexion showed white underneath and the manicured fingers clenched. Hannibal's shoulders began to hunch. "Damn you, cut it!" he snapped at the gorilla.

"That's right" said Cellini pleasantly. "And if I do anything to displease you just remember that you'll have to install a heating system here because you won't get your torrid Cobra back." He sauntered away.

For a while Cellini watched the wheels spin and the dice roll. It was difficult to tell whether the wheels were juiced, though with the Cobra and Lee Boyce running things it was a safe assumption that they were. It seemed a high class clientele and, on this night, they were certainly going in for a redistribution of wealth.

Cellini made for the card tables. Playing alone at a *21* table he sighted Abner Truman's niece Loraine Forrest. This then was what she did with her uncle's blank checks. He walked over.

The gash on her cheek was liberally smeared with face powder but it still stood out like a debutante on a bread line. She gave no sign of recognition as he stood beside her, watching her play.

Cellini asked: "Does your brother Carl spend his spare time around here too?"

"I don't give one hoot where my brother Carl or anyone else spends his spare time," was her measured reply.

She continued to play *21* listlessly, evincing as little interest when she won as when she lost. The dealer, a suave individual in dinner jacket, manipulated the cards with a competent dexterity. Good dealers are expensive but the Black Cat evidently realized that good dealers pay for themselves tenfold.

After a while, Cellini said: "It's safer to throw the bones in this kind of joint. It's a mistake to play this game here."

Loraine Forrest nodded. "I know."

Cellini indicated the dealer. "This baby is slick enough to give himself an ace and a picture any time you're winning a little too much."

"I don't care," she said.

"You're taking it too hard, kid. You've still got a swell figure." He wandered off.

LEE BOYCE, HANNIBAL and a bouncer with a white carnation in his lapel watched Cellini's every move with somber raging eyes—but they did nothing. Cellini smiled sweetly at them and walked over to a dice table. He found himself next to a beautifully-profiled picture actor who had yet to realize that he was poison at the box office.

Cellini said: "I caught your last picture. It came up to my expectations."

An eyebrow lifted in an appreciative and studied gesture. "Thank you, my man."

"In fact," pursued Cellini in a low tone, "if you ever want a chance to make another one I'll give you a tip."

"Indeed?" said the ham.

"Yes indeed. The tip is that the cops are down on this joint and anyone getting caught here will be out of luck. You'd better dust and pass the word to your friends to stay out of here."

"I will," said the actor fervently. "Thank you, my man."

The white-carnationed bouncer edged nearer, trying to eavesdrop. His clothing bulged every place. He evidently believed in defense preparedness.

"Stick to the Clover Club after this," Cellini cautioned the ham. "If you're caught in a raid here no one's going to get a hernia lifting your next option."

The picture star disappeared as if by magic. Cellini winked to White-carnation and moved on. He sighted a pair of double action doors and looked through. It was the kitchen. A deputy sheriff sat on a stool near the salad table, chewing away on some Kansas beef.

Cellini sidestepped a pretty shill who no doubt had a new system for beating the wheels and walked over to one of the roulette tables. He watched the play for some minutes and suddenly became bored. He reached down and in one heave upended the table, sending wheel, chips and money crashing to the floor.

The women yelped and gasped and the men swore as they scrambled over the floor after their money.

"It's a raid!" yelled Cellini.

Panic struck the bewildered players in full force. Instantly, a dozen fights broke out as they fought to cash in and get away. Someone next to Cellini grabbed him by the neck. Cellini twisted his body and hunched over, smashing the man's head against the edge of the upended table. The arms slipped from his neck.

"It's not a raid! Everybody keep cool!" It was Lee Boyce's voice striving to dominate the bedlam.

"Everybody's under arrest!" yelled Cellini.

Lee Boyce dashed into the kitchen. Somebody threw a bottle at Cellini that missed him and clipped a waiter over the ear. Patrons choked the doors.

Lee Boyce reappeared, dragging the deputy sheriff after him. With little zest, the sheriff called: "It ain't a raid, folks. I ought to know."

"Nobody move," shouted Cellini with full lungs. "You're all under arrest."

The sheriff began to protest again but by now the place was emptied of customers and outside sounded the whirr of self starters and the grinding of gears. Only Loraine Forrest remained unmoving and impassive on her stool by the card table. The deputy sheriff vanished discreetly.

Cellini dislodged a card caught under his lapel. He said: "I hope my friends don't do anything to the Cobra. They must be wondering what's taking me so long."

Lee Boyce's knuckles showed white and the small fists jerked spasmodically as he tried to control himself. Dealers, bouncers and shills surveyed the scene glumly. They were in an ugly mood.

Cellini heard a sound and he pivoted in time to catch one of the dealers charging him. He leaped sideways lightly, avoided a flailing fist, and sent his own lashing out. The blow caught the dealer over one ear and sent him skittering along the waxed floor.

THERE WAS A violent roar and a gun appeared in Hannibal's paw. Lee Boyce lunged for him, pinning his arms down.

"Pack it," commanded the gambler hoarsely.

Slowly, reluctantly, the gorilla returned the weapon to his pocket. Lee Boyce wiped his forehead with a monogrammed handkerchief. "All of you," he said, "leave that —— alone. The Cobra's not here and I'm giving orders. Just leave him alone. He'll be taken care of later."

Cellini nodded approval. He began edging for the side door. "Fine. And for the last time I'm telling you boys to get out of here and move some place else. Move while you still have some customers left because the next time I'll use a Flit gun."

"You just remember that if the Cobra doesn't get back here unharmed then—" Lee Boyce left the sentence dangling. A smug look settled on his face.

Instinct caused Cellini to whirl. Framed in the doorway, in all her feral beauty, was the Cobra. "So you thought I'd keep waiting for you," she said quietly.

Almost quicker than the eye could follow, her hand reached into the raven-black hair and came forward with one of those long hair pins. Cellini didn't move fast enough. Catlike, she leaped in a swirl of black satin and Cellini felt as if a long, hot poker had been driven into his left arm.

Cellini fell backwards and rolled over. He came up with

the automatic in his hand—freezing the sudden surge of movement toward him. His left arm hung limply at his side, throbbing with pain. He waved the gun in a semi-circle. "I'm leaving."

"Stop him," snapped the Cobra.

The bouncer with the white carnation suddenly spurted from Cellini's line of vision. Cellini continued to cover the others, not daring to turn.

"O.K.," said Lee Boyce with finality. "Drop that gun. You're finished."

White-carnation jammed his rod into the small of Cellini's back. "I'm countin' only one," said the bouncer. "Drop your heater."

Suddenly there was a blast and a spurt of flame and White-carnation dropped to the floor with a slug in his thigh. It had come from a tiny, pearl-handled revolver that Loraine Forrest held in her hand.

Cellini Smith and Loraine Forrest carefully backed out of the Black Cat.

Cellini Smith rolled back his shirt sleeve and examined the wound. He found it was superficial, the pin having pierced only the fleshy part of the arm. Though the painful throb persisted, the arm had lost its numbness. He bound the wound with a handkerchief and donned his jacket.

"Where's your car?" asked Cellini.

"I came in a taxi," replied Loraine Forrest. The excitement had rushed the blood to her face and the scar showed dull red in the lamplight.

"I'll drive you home." They made for the car. The small revolver was still in Loraine Forrest's hand. Now she put up the safety and dropped it into her handbag.

Cellini said: "I'd thank you for getting me out of that mess if I thought you wanted it."

"I don't. I just had the sudden urge to shoot somebody without getting into any trouble on account of it."

"Do you get that urge often?"

"Yes."

"Well, this time it came in handy. How come you're such a good shot?"

Her voice was steady and utterly sincere as she spoke. "I practice every day. I don't want to mess things up when I decide to kill myself."

They reached the car just as a sedan cut in front of them and braked short. Carl Forrest jumped out. His handsome visage was yellow with fright and his lips trembled as if from some terror. He ignored Cellini and grabbed his sister's arm urgently. "Loraine. Something's happened. It's Uncle Abner. He's been murdered!"

"So the old goat finally got it," remarked Loraine Forrest calmly.

3

Bloodletting

CELLINI ASKED: "WHAT happened?"

"How should I know?" moaned Carl Forrest. "I just saw him sitting there and I had to get out. I knew Loraine would be here so I came to get her."

"You didn't call the cops?"

Carl Forrest caught his breath. "No. I guess I should have. I was too shocked to think of anything like that."

"O.K.," said Cellini. "Get into your chariot and drive home. Your sister and I will follow in mine."

Carl Forrest nodded and returned to his sedan. Cellini and Loraine got into the coupé. Behind them the bounding cat in the neon sign suddenly went dark.

Cellini turned into Laurel Canyon again and began climbing up toward the Hollywood Hills. The girl next to him sat silently. The side of her face that he could see was unmarred but its beauty seemed chilling and unfeminine. He could not even gather a softening scent of perfume from her.

Finally, he asked: "Who gets Abner Truman's dough?"

"I do."

"All of it?"

"The old fool probably left a few hundred thousand to some dog foundation but I get the rest." She laughed hollowly. "A lot of good it'll do me now."

"How come your brother Carl isn't getting anything?"

She touched her scarred cheek with that characteristic, caressing gesture. "Uncle probably thought he could buy himself forgiveness for this by leaving me all his money. Besides, he regarded my brother as a wastrel. Carl always makes a beeline for very bad liquor and very beautiful women." Her voice became hard. "Why do even the scrawniest men expect to get the most beautiful women in the world? Can't they see anything else?"

"I'm sure I don't know," was Cellini's polite reply. He swerved past the gate and followed the sedan up the driveway.

Cellini Smith didn't bother to hunt for any pulsebeat but ran his fingers over the aged face. The flesh was cold and Abner Truman, as he sat at the desk in his study, wasn't waiting for any street car. A bullet had entered through his back and penetrated his heart, causing instant death.

"It's funny," said Loraine. "I don't even hate him any more." She lay curled on a sofa, a hand rubbing her disfigured cheek.

"Is this house in the city of L.A.?" asked Cellini.

Carl Forrest nodded an affirmative. He had steadied himself by now and was smoking a cigarette.

Cellini made for a phone and dialed Homicide with relish. It was a pleasure to rouse police dicks out of their beds at one in the morning. He spoke his piece, cradled the receiver and turned to Carl Forrest again.

"What time did you find your uncle dead?"

"Just before I ran to get Loraine."

"Well he must have died a few hours before. How come he was found so late when this place is lousy with servants?"

"That's the routine in this house," replied Carl Forrest. "If you noticed when we came in before there were no servants around. That's because my uncle always insisted they retire to their quarters after dinner was served."

"Where do they sleep?" asked Cellini.

"Down that way in the left wing of the house. After dinner they only stayed around if we had guests or if my uncle rang. But that was rare because my uncle was a very methodical man. He usually spent his evenings in the study here working on his papers and writing his diary."

Cellini walked over to the dead man again. Abner Truman was sitting with his head slumped over the desk and a quill pen in one hand. In front of him, a diary lay opened to that day. Abner Truman had noted the time of his entry—8:30 P.M.—and seven or eight lines before being killed. The entry concerned the hiring of a private investigator to oust the Black Cat from its premises.

LORAINE FORREST FOUND a deck of cards, pulled over a tea table and started on a game of solitaire. Cellini made a rapid survey of the room but could see no likely place for hiding the murder weapon.

Carl Forrest said: "Still you'd think the servants would have heard the shot. A silencer must have been used."

"Anything," replied Cellini. "A heavy piece of wool wrapped around the gun would have been enough. Are the doors locked at night?"

"Yes." Carl Forrest indicated the large French windows directly behind the dead man. "He must have come that way."

Cellini walked over to the wide-open windows. Below, he could see a cement walk that circled the entire house. He dropped over the window sill onto the walk. By the inadequate flame of a cigarette lighter, he searched the area immediately adjacent to the window. He could find nothing but the imprint of a heel that had misjudged the walk and stepped on the soft soil of a flower bed. He held the lighter closer. He could discern a line that cut through the center of the impression. It could have been made by a heel plate.

He heard, in the distance, the siren of an approaching prowl car. He hoisted himself over the sill, back into the study.

He walked over to the girl and said: "Hold your foot out."

Loraine Forrest extended a collector's item in leg. "Like them? They're very popular—at masquerades," she added bitterly.

"O.K., thanks." He nodded to Carl Forrest. "Now you."

A frown settled over the handsome face but he complied and showed the soles of his patent leather shoes. "What are you getting at?" he asked.

"It's all right," said Cellini. "Probably means nothing." He walked over to the desk and began paging through the diary. The entries were unrevealing, confined only to the prosaic events in the life of the late Abner Truman.

They heard the prowl car whine up the driveway and halt. A moment later two cops burst into the study. "Hey you!" yelled one of them.

Cellini put down the diary. "I know," he said. "We mustn't touch an itty bitty thing."

The cops barked orders, made phone calls, lumbered in and out of rooms opening closets and drawers and tarried over a bottle of Ballantine's they unearthed in an adjoining room. Aroused by the siren, servants in frayed negligee and bathrobe came and, with cold-creamed faces, peered at their dead master. After a while, they retired to the pantry for an orgy of horrified whispering.

Carl Forrest sat chain-smoking next to his sister. Cellini sank onto an ottoman beside them. He said: "Your uncle must have died shortly after he started on his diary. That was around eight-thirty and the shams will be asking where you were then. You better get your stories straight, both of you."

"What?!" exclaimed Carl Forrest. "You mean you have doubts as to who did it?"

Cellini admitted he had.

"You know damned well it's at your door."

"What," asked Cellini, "is at my door—besides the wolf?"

"The blame for this murder," said Carl Forrest. "You bungled that job at the Black Cat and let those gangsters know you were working for my uncle. Then they came and killed him. Nothing else could have happened."

"Maybe—but the Homicide men will still want to know where you were around eight-thirty."

"I was in my room all evening," snapped Carl Forrest. "I had a headache and it didn't stop. Shortly after midnight I came down because I thought a walk might do me good and I saw a light still on in my uncle's study. That's how I found him."

"Good," said Cellini. "No alibi is always a safe alibi. Even if you can't prove it the cops can't disprove it." He nodded to Loraine Forrest. "And you?"

"My alibi is just as safe," she replied without resentment. "I was driving around in the Valley until about ten and then I went to the Black Cat. Will it help you any if I add that since my accident I've hated my uncle more than anyone else?" She grimaced.

"That'll help a lot," he said drily.

"My God," cried Carl Forrest. "We sit here and gab. Why don't you do something, Smith?"

"There's nothing to do. Besides, my job is to get rid of the Black Cat and not to find Abner Truman's murderer."

CARL FORREST BIT his lips nervously. "Well you're through with that. I'm letting them stay there until their lease runs out. I don't want them to start gunning for me now."

Loraine Forrest nodded contemptuously toward her brother. "You'd think he had something to live for, wouldn't you?"

Cellini Smith said: "All right. I'll get off that job but I still have the thousand dollar retainer. Do you want me to stick around here for it and help if I can?"

"Yes," replied Carl Forrest. "Anything—but leave the Black Cat alone from now on."

Outside, they could hear a few cars rolling up the driveway. Loraine said to Cellini: "If you don't help around here—in fact if you do everything you can to help the murderer get clear, I'll give ten thousand dollars. It's all mine and I can afford it now, and where I'm going I won't need it."

Cellini shook his head slowly. "I bet you would spend ten G's for that," he said with a hint of admiration in his voice.

The door pushed open and the boys from Homicide, with equipment in their hands and sleep in their eyes, descended on the study like a horde of locusts. They worked seriously and efficiently. Abner Truman was an important corpse and they couldn't afford to bungle things.

Heading the Homicide contingent was Detective-sergeant Ira Haenigson. He was large, middle aged and soured on life in general and the seniority system in particular. His superiors weren't dropping dead with sufficient rapidity to suit him.

Haenigson ignored completely the corner where Cellini sat with the brother and sister. He barked at the shams who dusted and photographed and went into the pantry where he yelled questions at the help. He returned to the study and seemed to notice Cellini for the first time.

"Why don't somebody murder you for a change?" he asked.

"Your manners," said Cellini. "May I introduce Miss and Mr. Forrest. This tub of clues is Detective-sergeant Ira Haenigson."

"I know all about them," said the Homicide man. "What are you doing here?"

"I was on a job for the late Abner Truman."

"Are you mixed up with this murder?" Then he added inanely: "Direct or indirect?"

"Both ways," replied Cellini. "And the middle too. Only I was trying to keep it a secret for your birthday."

Ira Haenigson grunted. "O.K., Smith. Dust. I'll see you tomorrow."

Cellini Smith headed for the door when Haenigson's voice stopped him. "Just a moment. Where were you at eight-thirty tonight?"

"Oh, hell," said Cellini wearily. "Grow up." He slammed the door behind him.

IT WAS ONLY a few minutes before three in the morning when Cellini Smith bedded the coupé on a parking lot and walked across the street to his apartment building. He entered and went down the long, carpeted, first-floor hallway, halted at the last apartment door and fumbled for the key when he noticed a sheet of paper protruding from under the door.

He slipped it out. It proved to be a piece of his own stationery and the few penciled lines on it were in a neat and precise hand. They read:

We couldn't wait any longer. Next time we will. Do we wear formal for your funeral?

Cellini frowned and reread the message. Something was wrong. Obviously, the message came from Lee Boyce and it was equally obvious that Lee Boyce would never chance such a death threat, written in his own hand, getting to the police. Furthermore, it was not like the gambler to tire of waiting. Cellini grinned. He had it. The answer was simply that Boyce *was* waiting.

Cellini padded back silently and snapped off the night light in the hallway. He drew his automatic and returned in the darkness, inserted the key in the lock and threw the door wide open—dropping flat on the floor at the same instant.

A spat of blue-white flame cut through the blackness over Cellini's head. A moment of heavy silence and then Cellini heard the spurt of heavy, rushing feet. He lashed out with the barrel of the Colt and found a mark. Two hundred pounds thudded to the floor in the path of someone else who stumbled over him. Cellini struck again at a white blur. There was a cry and the blur disappeared.

Cellini stood up and snapped on his vestibule light. Hannibal lay on the floor, hugging an ankle. The sock and shoe were blood-soaked. Sprawling behind him, knocked cold, was Lee Boyce. One side of his face was a pulpy mess of blood and a trickle of carmine oozed from the corner of his mouth. The side of a Colt is messier than its business end but almost as useful.

Cellini pocketed two rods that lay on the floor then mixed himself a stiff whiskey. After a while, Hannibal began to swear, monotonously and repetitiously.

Cellini said: "Take that shoe off. The foot's going to swell."

The gorilla unlaced the shoe and pinpricks of sweat stood out on his face as he forced it off. The ankle seemed broken. Lee Boyce began to stir. Cellini saw a towel lying on the floor. It had a hole in the center and its frayed edges were singed black. He took it into the bathroom, wet it thoroughly and returned.

Lee Boyce was sitting up now. Cellini threw the towel to him. "Put that around your puss."

Cellini mixed himself another whiskey. He said to the gambler: "Take one of your shoes off and leave it here."

Lee Boyce swore thickly through the towel wrapped around his face. Cellini set down his drink. The gambler hurriedly worked a shoe off.

"That's better," approved Cellini. "I see you used that towel as a homemade silencer when you shot at me before. Where'd you get such a bright idea?"

The gambler's black eyes stared with unmoving hatred but he said nothing.

"I only ask," continued Cellini, "because the same bright idea was probably used when Abner Truman was killed a few hours ago. That is what is known as a clue."

Lee Boyce said something indistinguishable. The towel was reddening rapidly.

"That's right," said Cellini. "Abner Truman is the person you rented the Black Cat from. O.K., you two, beat it. You might as well stop gunning for me because I'm leaving your joint alone. And leave those shoes here."

Lee Boyce stood up and hauled Hannibal to his feet with difficulty. Cellini opened the apartment door. They stumbled out, the gorilla hopping on one foot, with an arm around the gambler's shoulders and Lee Boyce holding the blood-soaked towel to his face.

Cellini went to a window and waited till he saw the two figures emerge, struggle into a car and drive off. Then he placed the two guns he had collected into an old pillow case and set them in the hallway in front of his apartment. He locked the door from the inside and wedged a chair under the knob. He secured several water tumblers and balanced them inside the window shades where the slightest disturbance would send them shattering to the floor. Lee Boyce hadn't had much fight left in him but you don't need much to depress a trigger.

Cellini next went to the phone, dialed Abner Truman's home and asked for Ira Haenigson.

The detective-sergeant was still there.

Cellini said: "I'm leaving a couple of rods in front of my apartment door. Have someone pick them up and test them for the slug that fixed Truman."

"How'd you get them?"

"I clipped coupons from my breakfast cereal."

"O.K., Smith. And suppose you be here at ten sharp in the morning," Haenigson told him.

"On the dot," said Cellini and cradled the receiver.

Only then did Cellini Smith inspect the two shoes that were still on the floor. Hannibal's brogan was heavy and the sole and heel were both of rubber. In contrast, Lee Boyce's small shoe had leather heels and soles.

And in the heel of the gambler's shoe was a heel plate, for better traction on the Black Cat's waxed floor. Cellini did not have to take any measurements to know that the heel plate was identical with the one impressed in the flower bed of Abner Truman's erstwhile home.

4

Fall-Guy Wanted

IT WAS TWELVE thirty the following afternoon when Cellini Smith was awakened by the ringing of his telephone. He washed and dressed slowly, allowing the phone to ring, and after a while it stopped. Completely clothed, he secured the Colt from under his pillow and left.

An hour later he talked his way through the gents of the press and the police guarding Abner Truman's home. He found Detective-sergeant Ira Haenigson straining a wicker chair on the veranda, surrounded by a few of his department men.

"Where in hell have you been?" roared the Homicide man. "I been phoning your apartment and office all morning."

Cellini selected a chair and sat down. "I've been up all night following a couple of leads for you that didn't pan out."

Haenigson grunted doubtfully and snapped at the department men: "Find some work to do. Go on the roof where you can see her better but get out of here." The men retreated inside the house. "What a bunch," continued Haenigson. "Now they're trying to get a girl show with each murder."

"How come?" asked Cellini.

"It's that crazy niece."

"Loraine Forrest?"

"Uh huh. She's taking a swim in the pool down there with no clothes on. She says she don't give a damn and that it's her house and that besides no one would look at her if she paid them. She'll be singing another tune before I get through with this case."

"So you think she did it?"

"Hell, yes," snorted Haenigson. "She's as odd as Dick's hatband. She hated her uncle because of the accident to her pan. She says herself she hated him enough to kill him and she got a swiss cheese alibi. I talked with Truman's lawyer this morning and she gets most of the estate."

"You think the motive is money?"

"I can't figure it any other way. How about you?"

Cellini shook his head. In the distance, he saw the unclothed, white figure of the girl as she calmly crossed from the swimming pool to the rear of the house. He asked: "Those two rods I sent you. How'd they check?"

"No dice. Smith, I need a fall-guy bad. Abner Truman rated pretty high and this thing is getting hotter than Dutch love. You got to come clean with anything that can help me."

"I thought you had Loraine Forrest tabbed."

"Sure, but I have to be open minded. Besides, it would be tough sledding to prove she did it. She's no dope and she's got enough dough now to hire the supreme court."

"How about the servants?"

"Nothing doing. They ain't even servants. They call themselves family retainers."

"Then what about Lee Boyce and the Cobra?"

"Yeah," said Haenigson. "I heard about how you were mixed up with that angle. It's time you gave me your story."

For fifteen minutes, Cellini recounted all that had occurred. Carl Forrest came out to the veranda and sat down beside them. His eyes were bloodshot and, with his uncle's restraining influence gone, he was quite drunk on brandy.

When Cellini had finished, Haenigson said: "That meshes with what I heard but it still don't give us our fall-guy."

Cellini jerked a finger at Carl Forrest. "How about him?"

Truman's nephew suddenly bolted upright. "Say, what are you trying to pull off here?"

Haenigson shook his head slowly. "He got no alibi but it's hard to see any motive because that nutty skirt gets the dough."

Carl Forrest began to hammer on his knees. "I asked what you're trying to pull off!"

Cellini said: "Of course, he might be figuring that his sister would finally kill herself the way she's promised and then he'd finally inherit everything."

The detective-sergeant shrugged. "From all I can figure, this guy don't care much for money—just wine and women."

It required sixty seconds, Cellini calculated, for Carl Forrest to tell him and Haenigson exactly where to go before he lammed into the house.

Ira Haenigson smiled. "Think it helped?"

"No," said Cellini. "He's tougher than he looks."

The detective-sergeant stood up. "Guess I'll run down to the Black Cat with a few of the boys. Coming along?"

"Maybe later."

"O.K., Smith, but watch your step. If you're holding out on me in this case the only place your license will do you any good will be in the bathroom."

CELLINI SMITH WAITED till he saw the department cars speed down the driveway, then got up and walked around the side of the house till he reached the study window. He kneeled over the heel-print that he had discovered the night before in the flower bed. The shams hadn't missed it either for grey traces clung to the edges of the print. They had already taken a plaster negative of the impression.

Cellini retraced his steps and went inside the house where he found a phone. He rang information, secured the number of the Black Cat and dialed again. To the voice that responded, he said: "This is Cellini Smith. Tell Lee Boyce the shams will be around there in a few minutes to see if they can prove he killed Abner Truman." Then he hung up.

A voice asked: "Do the police think Lee Boyce killed my uncle?"

Cellini turned to confront Loraine Forrest. She wore slacks with her hair dressed low in an ineffectual attempt to conceal the scar. "No," he replied. "They're just checking. They think you did it."

She laughed without parting her lips. "And what do you think?"

"I don't know yet but if that gun you helped me out with at the Black Cat is the one that killed your uncle then you better let me take care of it."

"Nothing doing," said Loraine Forrest. "Just keep wondering. Maybe it'll help confuse things."

"O.K. I'm going down to the Black Cat. Want to tag along?"

Loraine Forrest nodded and they went out to the coupé and headed down the winding grade for the Valley.

After a while, Loraine asked: "Why did you call Lee Boyce and tell him the cops were coming over?"

"It's an old gag," replied Cellini. "It didn't hurt Haenigson any because he couldn't get anything out of an egg like Lee

Boyce with a stomach pump. And this way Lee Boyce thinks I did him a favor and he might trust me."

"Do you think Boyce killed my uncle?"

"There's a good chance. He left his shoe print outside your uncle's study last night."

"I see," she said. "If I thought it were true I could really like him."

Fifteen minutes later, Cellini Smith cut into the Black Cat's parking lot. They entered the gambling joint by the rear door to find a half dozen Homicide men prowling the place. Another was fanning Lee Boyce, and others who worked there, with no success. Cellini's warning had given them time to ditch their artillery.

Detective-sergeant Haenigson was grilling the Cobra. She said: "I tell you I don't know a damn thing about your Abner Truman."

"Where were you between eight forty-five and nine fifteen last night?" asked Haenigson.

The Cobra's jet-black eyes found Cellini Smith and she stabbed a finger at him. "Ask that guy. I was driving to Hollywood and Vine to meet him."

"That's right," said Cellini.

"The hell it is," snorted Ira Haenigson. "All you know is you made an appointment to meet her but how do you know she didn't go up to Truman instead of to Hollywood and Vine?"

"She wouldn't do that," replied Cellini, "because she didn't know I wasn't waiting to meet her there."

"Since when do you go around making alibis for every round-heel?"

CELLINI SHRUGGED. HE saw a pair of dice and rolled them. They turned up a deuce.

"And how about you?" asked the Homicide man of the no longer dapper Lee Boyce.

The side of the gambler's face that Cellini had hit was completely covered with adhesive. He said: "After I had dinner last night I went to the office upstairs and had a nap on the couch. No one was with me but everybody saw me go up and I came down around nine thirty or a little after."

"Do you own this place?" asked Haenigson.

"Half of it." He nodded to the Cobra. "We're fifty-fifty partners in this outfit."

"Most of the guys working around here have been with you for a long time, haven't they?"

"I get it," said Lee Boyce. "Well, you're right. They'd back up any alibi of mine. I could even have dropped out of the office window to the parking lot and nobody would have known. But the point is I had no reason to kill Abner Truman."

"He hired Smith here to get you out."

The gambler took a long time before responding. "So that's what he wanted," he finally said.

"You didn't know?"

Lee Boyce shook his head. "No. So I could have no reason for wanting to kill Abner Truman. I thought Smith was trying to cut in on us."

Carl Forrest came in from the bar, a drink in his hand.

"What the hell is this?" asked Haenigson. "A meeting hall?"

"Whatever it is," replied Forrest coolly, "my sister owns it and I have a right to be here."

"Nobody has a right to be in a place like this."

The Cobra framed her teeth in a beguiling smile. "You're not going to get us closed up!"

Haenigson shrugged. "It's none of my business but it's a hell of a town that lets a place like this operate wide open."

The Cobra went up close to the Detective-sergeant. "But we're on the level and there are lots of other gambling houses."

"It's none of my business," repeated Haenigson stolidly. "I just want to find out who killed Abner Truman."

The Cobra put her arms around Ira Haenigson's neck. "I knew you'd understand," she said with a husky trill.

The detective-sergeant reddened as one of his men tittered. "If you play square with me on Abner Truman," he began weakly.

Suddenly the Cobra dropped her arms and pushed him away. "You and your damned stinking Abner Truman!" she screamed. "Where the hell do you get the idea you can come in here and pin a murder rap on us?" She leaped at the detective-sergeant and began to claw him with pantherlike fury.

Cellini Smith began to laugh.

The Cobra began to kick at Haenigson's legs and pummel his face and body with clenched fists. He backed and managed to dive behind the safety of a roulette table.

Lee Boyce strode up to the Cobra and delivered a smashing, backhand slap. "What's the idea of getting their fur up against us?" he snarled.

The Cobra stumbled backwards. She seemed to fear this small, dapper gambler far more than any detective of Homicide. She replied meekly: "I just don't like the way he takes it for granted we're mixed up in the murder. He thinks—"

"Button your pan!"

"Yes, Lee."

"See here," put in Carl Forrest. "You got no call to slap a lady and talk to her like that."

"You get out." Lee Boyce spoke without raising his voice but Carl Forrest turned abruptly and walked out with quick, jerky steps.

Cellini Smith tried again and drew another deuce. Ira Haenigson came out from behind his refuge, mopping the red threads that the Cobra's fingernails had left on his cheeks. His lips trembled with rage and he moved toward the Cobra— but suddenly he stopped short as one of his men hurried in, bearing a pair of slim, tan shoes.

THE COP CONFINED himself to a significant nod as he handed the shoes to Haenigson. "Where did you find them?" asked the detective-sergeant eagerly.

"They were hid in a closet in the upstairs office."

Cellini walked over and examined them. The heel of one bore an encrusted ring of soil and embedded in each was a heel plate.

"What now?" asked Lee Boyce suspiciously. "Everybody's going in the shoe business."

Ira Haenigson was suddenly calm and good-humored. He examined the shoes without bothering about the tiny ooze of blood that coursed down his cheek and neck and under his collar. "They're nice," he commented. "Cost a lot?"

"Thirty-two a pair," replied the gambler.

"Then you admit they're yours?"

"Sure, they're mine. What of it?"

"It's interesting," said Haenigson. "Where did you get such

pretty shoes?"

"They're custom made. All mine are."

"Mmmm," said the detective-sergeant happily. "These metal cleats or plates or whatever they are in the heels. What are they for?"

"I have them put in all my shoes so I don't slide over the floor." There was now a note of bewildered anxiety in Lee Boyce's voice.

"How ducky. Well I think they'll slide you right into a wooden overcoat."

Lee Boyce stayed silent. The Cobra emitted a hissing sound. "I told you, Lee. They're trying to frame you."

"Let them try." The gambler lit a cigarette and flipped the match toward the Homicide man. "How come that crack about a wooden overcoat?"

Ira Haenigson said: "You left your heelprint in the dirt right outside Abner Truman's study window when he was shot last night."

"That's a lie."

"The jury won't think so. We took a plaster impression and the plate in the heel came up clear as noodle soup. It's a dead giveaway."

"You damned flatfoot," muttered Lee Boyce. "I said it's a lie. What would I want to kill that Truman for?"

"Plenty reason," replied Haenigson. "Cellini Smith came here yesterday afternoon and you guessed that Abner Truman was trying to get you out so you went up there last night. They keep the gate open at night so you walked right through and around to the study window. You're sunk, Boyce. Why don't you whistle and we'll make it painless?"

"Nothing doing," said Lee Boyce. "You're not tagging me for a rap like this." He moved with unhurried steps for the door that gave onto the parking lot.

"Cut it!" barked Haenigson. "You know better. You'll be plugged before you reach that door. You haven't even got a rod on you."

The moment of silence that followed was broken by Loraine Forrest. "A difference of opinion, Mr. Haenigson. I think he will reach that door." The small, pearl-handled revolver was again in her hand and despite its toylike appearance none of the men seemed inclined to dispute with it.

"Good girl," said Lee Boyce.

"You loony twist!" yelled Haenigson. "That guy murdered your own uncle."

"More power to him. That's why I'm doing this."

The veins began to stand out on the detective-sergeant's neck. "You young idiot!" he roared. "You're letting yourself in for a felony!" He turned to his men. "Get Boyce. She won't shoot."

Loraine Forrest took a few steps and planted herself in front of the gambler. "I will too shoot," she said with dead calm.

Several of the men had guns in their hand now but the girl prevented them from getting a bead on the gambler. Loraine Forrest and Lee Boyce began to back out. One of the dicks hunched low and started to charge after the girl.

Cellini Smith never knew why he did it but he automatically put his foot out and the dick went sprawling over the floor.

As the tiny revolver kept the Homicide men at bay, Cellini opened the door, waited till the girl and the gambler had backed out, then stepped out after them and slammed it shut.

5

Death-Watch

CELLINI SMITH, LEE Boyce and Loraine Forrest sprinted for the coupé. They reached it without hindrance. Cellini jumped behind the wheel, the girl sat in on the other side and then Lee Boyce wedged himself in. Just as they skidded out of the parking lot a cautious dick opened the rear door of the Black Cat and sent futile shots after them.

Cellini screeched around a corner and, pushing his heap to its limit, began cutting in and out of side streets.

Lee Boyce lit two cigarettes and handed one to Loraine Forrest. "Good girl," he said again.

Not too far away, they could hear the sirens of police cars begin wailing. Cellini said: "Too bad we haven't got a radio to check on them. I'll head out of the county for Bakersfield till it gets dark."

The gambler shook his head. "Go around the block and turn back to Ventura Boulevard."

"Hell, no. The shams will be currycombing that whole area." The small revolver was still in Loraine Forrest's hand. She jammed it against Cellini's ribs. "Do as he says."

Cellini shrugged. He cut to the left on the next corner and headed back, with the sirens coming in louder.

"Go to the corner," instructed Lee Boyce, "and turn right. You'll see a drive-in a couple of lots down. Head into it slowly."

"That's better," nodded Cellini. "I thought you were giving

yourself up like in books." He turned the corner and a few seconds later casually tooled into the drive-in and cut the motor.

A carhop looking like a Radio City usherette bore down on them. Loraine Forrest covered the revolver she held against Cellini's side with her purse.

"Nice day," said the waitress.

"It stinks," said Lee Boyce. "Get three ham sandwiches and three coffees."

The carhop went away. Behind them prowl cars, their sirens wide open, raced by. Cellini indicated the revolver. "If you must do that, do it gently. You don't have to cave in my ribs."

"It stays right there," was her terse reply.

"You got guts, baby," said Lee Boyce admiringly. "Too bad we never met before."

"It takes a murderer to get romantic about me." She gave a hollow laugh. "What'll we do about him?"

"Smith? I don't know. We'll feed him to the crocodiles if he gets tough."

"I don't think he will. He helped us get away."

"Yeah," said the gambler. "They all stink but I can't figure this one out." He patted his adhesive-covered cheek. "Last night he gave me this and today he plays pals."

"How did you get it?" asked the girl.

"He socked me with a rod. I'll pay him off yet."

"Is it bad?"

"It took twelve stitches. The sawbones told me it'll always show."

"We'd make a perfect pair," she said distantly. "You're right—it's too bad we never met before."

The carhop brought the food, commented on all the police cars careening past them on the boulevard and went away.

Cellini said: "It's nice to hear you milkheads discussing what to do with me but let's decide what Boyce is going to do."

"Muffle it," said the gambler.

The girl tapped Cellini's ribs with the revolver. "You'd better do as we tell you."

"He's packing a rod," said Lee Boyce.

"The left side."

Loraine Forrest reached over with her right hand, removed Cellini's Colt and passed it to the gambler. He broke it, checked the loading and contentedly dropped it into his pocket.

"Did you really kill my uncle?" asked Loraine.

"No."

"Oh." There was a note of disappointment in her voice. "You know I helped you because I thought you had and deserved to get away with it."

"You're a pinhead, sister," commented Lee Boyce, "but you're O.K. I'll dust now. There's a couple of things I've got to do. Don't let Smith move for a half hour."

The sun had set and it was now rapidly growing darker. For several minutes there had been no sound of sirens. The police had probably decided they were far away by now and had deployed in all directions in their fruitless search.

The gambler gulped down his coffee, set the cup on the tray and opened the car door. "Take it easy," he said to the girl. For a few moments they could see the white, receding patch of adhesive that covered a side of his face and then he was out of sight.

CELLINI SMITH FINISHED his sandwich under the

never relaxing pressure of the gun barrel. "Do you realize," he finally asked, "that you and I have abetted and aided a criminal to escape?"

"I don't care about that, Mr. Smith. Just stay quiet for a half hour."

"Suppose I don't want to?"

"Then I'll shoot you, Mr. Smith. Really I will. I've told you I don't intend living long anyway so I don't care."

"You ought to stay out of this kind of thing," said Cellini. "You're just not made for it."

"What do you mean?"

"You've been threatening the whole police department and everybody else with that popgun in your hand but you never remembered to put the safety off. I'm surprised Haenigson didn't notice it."

She looked at the revolver and laughed. It sounded almost normal to Cellini.

"Why didn't you take it away from me?" she asked.

"It's just a hunch I have," he replied.

"But won't you lose your license for helping Lee Boyce to get away?"

"I'll try not to. Boyce has to be free for me to have a chance to work my idea out."

She handed him the small revolver. "Here. I guess I'd better let you take care of it."

It was now dark enough for Cellini's purposes. He tooted the carhop, paid the check and the trays were removed. He asked: "How long does it take to drive from your house to the Black Cat?"

"Fifteen or twenty minutes, depending on the traffic."

"How many ways can you make the trips within that approximate time?"

"There are about three or four routes," said Loraine Forrest.

Cellini pressed the starter and engaged the clutch. "Fine. Let's start with the shortest and quickest way. Show me how you'd drive there."

Following the girl's directions, Cellini cut across Ventura Boulevard, into Acorn and they began to climb. He drove slowly, carefully watching the passing scenery by moon and occasional lamp light. He watched stores and real estate offices yield to auto camps and small cottages which in turn gave way to barren, mountainous country as they ascended.

Some fifteen minutes later they hove into sight of the late Abner Truman's home. Cellini turned the car around. "That's far enough," he said. "Now show me the next quickest way to get to the Black Cat."

Loraine Forrest directed him off to a wide, concrete grade. They rolled downward, past Spanish stuccoed bungalows and colonial homes. As they descended to the Valley, there were truck farms and small walnut ranches.

They reached Ventura Boulevard again. Cellini stopped by a liquor store and bought a pint bottle of whiskey. He returned to the car and turned it around. "Now the next way," he said.

They rode in silence till they neared the crest of the hill when Cellini suddenly pulled over to the shoulder and braked. "What's that?"

"What's what?" asked Loraine.

He pointed. "Down there."

She leaned out. By the light of a three-quarter moon she could see a deep gully and the formless shadows of scrub and desert vegetation several hundred feet down.

"There's nothing there," said Loraine Forrest. "That's just a ravine between those two hills."

"I know," he said impatiently. "I made a wild guess. What is it called?"

"Lobego Canyon."

"Lobego Canyon. Fine. Forget the other routes. Now are you willing to string along with me without being a nuisance?"

"Sure. What have I got to lose?"

"Just your head blown off."

She stroked the scar on her cheek. "That would only help me. Let's go."

"O.K. Now just show me how we can reach your house without being seen. Around the back way."

Loraine Forrest nodded. They followed narrow, winding dirt roads till, some minutes later, they found themselves in back of the Truman house.

CELLINI SMITH AND Loraine Forrest made their way through fruit trees, over gardens and past tennis courts and the swimming pool.

"Are there any dogs in the house?" asked Cellini.

She shook her head. "Only two-legged ones."

Hugging the shadows, Cellini led the way around the side of the house. Finally they reached a large, protecting cluster of poinsettias. "We'll stay here, Miss Forrest. It may be a long wait."

"If you call me Loraine I won't blush."

"You're God's gift to the psychoanalysts, Loraine. Don't talk so loud."

They crouched behind the flowers, their eyes searching the surrounding darkness, their ears straining for some foreign sound. Some twelve or fifteen feet in front of them they could see the window that gave into Abner Truman's study. The lamp on the desk was lit but there was no one visible inside the room.

Lights were on in most of the other rooms and shadows constantly crossed back and forth. They could hear the distant murmur of voices and grinding gears from in front of the house. Cellini produced the pint bottle, broke the label and tinfoil capping and drank from it before passing it to the girl.

The ceiling light in the study was snapped on, casting a yellow circle of light on the lawn and flower beds in front of them. The boxed figure of Detective-sergeant Ira Haenigson entered their line of vision and sat down at the desk. He opened the desk drawers and riffled through some papers. Even from where Cellini stood he could see that impatience and frustration, rather than any hope of discovery, had driven the Homicide man to reexamine the contents of Abner Truman's desk.

Forrest and the Cobra appeared in front of the window. With characteristic thoroughness, Haenigson had thought it best to have everybody in one place where he could keep his good eye on them.

The Cobra seemed angry as her mouth moved in speech and the long fingernails pointed at Haenigson. The detective-sergeant stood up and went around to the safety of the other side of the desk. A few more moments of argument and he left.

"Lee Boyce is the only one who can handle that—" whispered Loraine.

Carl Forrest and the Cobra were talking now. Again it seemed like an argument.

"Boyce would sock her but my brother will try to flatter her," said Loraine.

"Shut up and drink," replied Cellini.

In a short while, Loraine proved to be right. Carl Forrest took the Cobra in his arms and kissed her. She didn't struggle much. Abruptly they broke apart and Forrest wiped his lips with a handkerchief as they evidently heard footsteps.

Again Ira Haenigson entered and Forrest and the Cobra sat down on a couch beyond the desk. The detective-sergeant drew a chair up close and obviously started to throw the book at them. Department men crossed back and forth and occasionally a servant showed up with drinks or a tray of food.

Cellini brought the bottle to his lips when suddenly he grew rigid. The orb of light coming from the study window had suddenly vanished.

A figure had come between them and the study window.

They watched the figure as it silently moved closer to the house. When it was within three or four feet of the house an arm dipped into clothing and then came up. Cellini dropped the whiskey bottle and plunged madly through expensive gardening.

At the instant that Cellini crashed into the figure, a gun boomed off, shattering glass and echoing through the surrounding hills.

FIVE MINUTES LATER they were all assembled in the study. Carl Forrest and the Cobra stood discreetly silent at one side, awaiting developments. Loraine Forrest sat behind the desk fingering the scar and gazing sardonically at each in turn. Lee Boyce, the figure that had padded up to the study window, lay unconscious on the couch, and next to him, a cop nursed the bruised knuckles that had sent the gambler to sleep.

Ira Haenigson strode back and forth nervously. "I hate to do it, Smith," he finally said.

"You hate to do what?" asked Cellini.

"To step on you—but I got to do it. I hope you don't have to go to the pen. Maybe you'll just lose your license."

"You're so good and big," cooed Cellini.

The Homicide man pointed to a bullet hole in the wall near where he and Carl Forrest had sat. "Smith, you saved my life before by throwing off Boyce's aim when he tried to gun me from outside and I appreciate it. But that still don't alter the fact that you helped Boyce get away."

"Don't let your conscience worry you," said Cellini, "because I saved you from nothing. Lee Boyce wasn't shooting at you."

"Sure. He was just trying to part my hair. Lee Boyce is a killer. He got Abner Truman and when I tagged him for it he tried to get me."

"Lee Boyce is a killer all right but he didn't kill Abner Truman last night and he wasn't trying to get you tonight."

"Who was he shooting at, then?"

The gambler on the couch stirred and slowly sat up. The cop next to him stepped closer and Boyce stayed quiet.

Cellini said: "Here's the way I see it and Boyce will tell you if I'm wrong. The Cobra was his squaw. And, as the Cobra is no Vassar girl, she knew Boyce was a killer and knew what would happen if she tried to leave him. The Cobra was tired of him but was too scared to do anything about it." He nodded to the Cobra. "Am I right?"

"Go to hell, you lousy dick."

Cellini shrugged. "That's her way of saying I'm right. Anyway, she met up with Carl Forrest and they went for each other but were afraid to do anything about it on account of Boyce. So they decided to kill two birds with one bullet. They figured out a way to take over the Black Cat and get rid of Boyce at the same time."

"Are we going to listen to that crazy hophead?" demanded Carl Forrest.

"Sure we will," said Ira Haenigson.

"Forrest took care of his uncle's realty holdings," continued Cellini, "and rented that place in the Valley to Boyce and the Cobra. Then he went and told his uncle about it and they decided to hire me to get the Black Cat out of there. That done, Carl Forrest killed his uncle and framed Boyce for the killing by planting the heelprint of one of his shoes outside the window here. The Cobra must have swiped the shoe for that purpose. After the murder, Forrest told me to forget about the Black Cat. Even if he didn't get his uncle's money he figured that he got the Cobra and a good business in the Black Cat. Boyce would take the murder rap and there was always a good chance his sister would kill herself and he'd get everything."

Carl Forrest laughed unsurely. "I'll see that two-bit operative gets blown out of this town."

HAENIGSON STROKED HIS chin. "Smith," he said slowly, "if you can prove it, I'll forget you were accessory to an escape."

"You're damned right you'll forget it," replied Cellini, "because I had to have Boyce free, where you couldn't work on him, to prove my idea. I knew Boyce would get the same idea

I did and would come back here and try to kill Forrest. That's who he was gunning for. Is that right?"

The gambler nodded.

"But you can't prove it," said Forrest harshly, "because it's all a frame."

Cellini said: "I've got plenty of proof. The first time I told the Cobra my name was when I phoned her last night and asked her to meet me at Hollywood and Vine. Yet she knew who I was because Carl Forrest had told her he and his uncle were hiring me to set up the window dressing for the murder."

"You poor fool," said the Cobra good-naturedly. "I just remembered your voice. You were at the Cat that afternoon in case you forget."

"Maybe," replied Cellini, "but I've got something better. Forrest killed his uncle around eight-thirty, then went up to his room and came down to find the body officially. Instead of calling the police he went down to the Black Cat."

Carl Forrest said: "I told you that was because I was scared and I wanted to get my sister."

"The hell you were scared. You just tried to get rid of the murder weapon. I've got a friend of mine who's a scoutmaster and I had him put a couple of hundred of his kids to work searching. A little while ago they phoned me to say they found the gun in Lobego Canyon where you threw it from your car on your way down to the Black Cat."

It was a telling blow. Carl Forrest paled and his hands began to shake. "You fool," screamed the Cobra. "You damned awful fool!" She leaped for him and a couple of cops jumped to separate them.

Loraine Forrest stood up and walked out to the pantry. Carl

Forrest and the Cobra were dragged away.

"I guess you were right," said Haenigson glumly.

Loraine returned with a drink. Cellini reached for it but she walked right by him and handed it to Lee Boyce. He took it and downed it in one swallow.

"You said I have guts," she told him. "I also have a lot of money and that ought to count with you. Do you think we might make a go of it together?"

"Maybe," said the gambler. "Don't rush me."

She touched the scar. "That is if you don't mind looking at me with this."

"I can always stand on the other side, sister."

Cellini swore. "This romantic atmosphere is getting me down. I want a drink."

He started for the pantry but Haenigson's voice arrested him. "Smith, have your scouting friends send me that rod—without a lot of kiddies' prints on it."

Cellini grimaced. "*You're* my scouting friend, sweetheart, and you better send your own kiddies into Lobego Canyon—because that's where it is."

Bail Bait

Jimmy Legg was guilty as hell—and there were witnesses to prove it. So—why did the worthy Judge Reynolds dismiss the D.A.'s case against the little cracksman? The answer was a surprise even to the shockproof Cellini—paid real dough for the first time in his checkered career to explain why Justice was deaf and dumb as well as stone blind.

1

Justice For Sale

HE CHECKED A curved wrist watch that you knew he couldn't have come by honestly and found that it was just two minutes short of nine in the morning. Chewing away at the toothpick between his thin, slitted lips, he entered the Hall of Justice.

His colorless eyes surveyed the signs and arrows on the walls of the vaulted vestibule. Coroner, Traffic, Small Claims, Bail—there were dozens. He read them all and when he didn't find what he wanted he walked over to the elevator starter.

"Reynolds." He spoke the word without moving the toothpick.

"Huh?" asked the starter.

"Reynolds," he repeated. "Where do I find the guy?"

"Oh, you mean *Judge* Reynolds."

"I know what I mean. Where do I find him?"

The starter named a floor and office number and he entered a waiting elevator. Other passengers pushed in, crowding him to the back. A big man, well-cushioned with fat, squeezed him to the wall but suddenly stiffened. The fat man wasn't sure, but he thought he felt something hard and unyielding—something like a gun—over the other one's chest. The fat man swung around to find himself looking into the colorless eyes. The fat man swallowed heavily, said nothing, and got off at the first stop.

He left the elevator four stops later and walked down the hall till he found the door he wanted. He pushed through without knocking. An elderly man sat alone behind a desk, robed in judicial black.

He spat out the toothpick and asked: "You Reynolds?"

"Yes," replied the jurist. "What can I do for you?"

"Plenty. My handle is Manny Simms."

"Yes?"

Manny Simms reached into his breast pocket and tossed an envelope onto the glass top. "Look at that first, Reynolds."

The judge removed a rubber band from the envelope and emptied its contents on the blotter. It was a packet of twenty-dollar bills.

"Count them, Reynolds."

The judge frowned. "Mr. Simms, I want to be certain before I do something about it. Are you trying to bribe me?"

Simms ignored the question. "There's fifty slices of that lettuce there—just one grand—and you can buy a lot of gavels with that. You got a case coming up in your court this morning. A guy called Jimmy Legg." Manny Simms shoved another toothpick into his face before continuing. "That grand, Reynolds, is to let Jimmy Legg go."

AN HOUR LATER, at precisely ten o'clock, Judge Reynolds left his chambers, crossed the hall, and passed through a door that gave into the rear of Magistrate's Court, Division Six.

The bailiff saw him coming and intoned: "Los Angeles County Magistrate's Court Division Six the Honorable Frank Reynolds presiding rise please sit down please thank you quiet everybody."

The crowd in the courtroom made a half-hearted gesture toward standing up as His Honor entered with dignified steps and sat behind the massive, elevated desk.

Reynolds fitted pince-nez to his razorback nose and thumbed through the mound of papers before him. They concerned the cases that were scheduled for hearing that day. He read the first sheet carefully, scanned through several of the following, then nodded to the clerk.

The clerk called the first case. A henpecked husband had gone berserk and forced his mother-in-law to eat his marriage certificate and had then proceeded to beat her with a telephone. The husband pled not guilty and Reynolds remanded him for trial. The second, third, and fourth cases were disposed of with equal rapidity. It was hardly ten twenty by the clock when the case of James Legg was called.

Jimmy Legg stood up and gazed at His Honor with all the

doe-eyed innocence that a two-time loser can muster. Beside him stood Howard Garrett, one of the better mouthpieces, a comforting hand on his client's shoulder. Garrett gave the impression that this thing would make the Dreyfus case look like a traffic violation. A young, pimply-faced deputy district attorney rose for the state. He had Jimmy Legg dead to rights and he sounded very bored.

Legg, it seemed, had jimmied his way into the Lansing Investment Company, at the Tower Building, two nights before and had souped open the office safe. The janitor of the building heard the detonation and rushed up to be sapped for his pains. Legg made good his escape after slugging a screaming stenographer who was returning for some papers she'd forgotten.

Through a thumbprint on the outside door jamb of the Lansing offices, the police were able to identify Legg and haul him in two days later. Both janitor and stenographer picked Jimmy Legg out of a lineup as the man who had assaulted them. The deputy D.A. concluded the bare recital by asking for an early trial.

Judge Reynolds regarded the accused. It was an open and shut case but Legg looked jaunty and confident. Howard Garrett, his attorney, pled not guilty. Legg was a victim of circumstances, the lawyer nearly sobbed. That thumbprint was on the door because Legg had gone up earlier that day to invest some money. As for the identification by janitor and stenographer—who knew what sinister forces were behind this whole thing?

Judge Reynolds asked several perfunctory questions. He didn't seem very interested in the replies but seemed, rather, to be debating something within himself. Finally, he buried his nose in the papers before him and said in a low voice: "Insufficient evidence for trial. Release the accused."

The deputy laughed. His Honor was some joker!

"I was not aware of my reputation for wit," flared Judge Reynolds. "I said there was insufficient evidence to waste the taxpayers' money on a trial."

The pimples on the deputy's face reddened. "Insufficient—"

"Enough of this," snapped His Honor. "Next case."

A hiss of shocked astonishment passed over the courtroom. The deputy sat down weakly, staring at the judge in dumbfounded wonder. Even James Legg could hardly believe his good fortune and stood without moving till Garrett grabbed him by the arm and hustled him out.

More cases were called. White-faced, his hands clenched tensely, Reynolds handed down his decisions. It was some thirty minutes later when he rapped for silence and said: "Clerk, what time is it?"

The clerk checked. "Five minutes past eleven, Your Honor."

"In that case I should like to interrupt these proceedings to explain my behavior in freeing James Legg who should patently have been held for trial."

The pimple-faced deputy D.A. swore softly under his breath. A couple of reporters sat up straight, their noses twitching at the scent of a headline.

"This morning at nine," continued the judge, "I received a visitor in my chambers. He introduced himself as one Manny Simms, and offered to bribe me if I freed James Legg. Naturally, I refused and sent out an alarm but he escaped. When I later entered court I found this paper on my bench. Clerk, read it aloud."

The judge passed it down. The clerk's voice sounded strange in the hushed room as he read aloud the scrawled writing. "I'm hiding under your desk and I've got a rod on your belly so you better not move from the desk. Do as I tell you. Let Jimmy Legg go and give him a half-hour start. Not a second less if you want to live." The clerk looked up. "It is signed, Manny Simms."

A swelling murmur swept the courtroom and the bailiff called for silence. Judge Reynolds stood up and passed a weary hand over his eyes. He said: "Perhaps I should not have considered my own life so valuable. I don't know. At any rate, bailiff, arrest that man hiding under the bench."

Manny Simms stepped out and viewed the courtroom with a sardonic smile. The toothpick in his mouth was now soft and pulpy. He laid the gun in his hand on the bench. "O.K., Reynolds. You followed orders. I ain't kicking."

A FREE MAN, Jimmy Legg left the Hall of Justice with Howard Garrett, his attorney, at his side. The lawyer was frowning. "Jimmy, you must have been born with a gold horseshoe in your mouth."

"The judge knew I was innocent," declared Legg with a grin.

"I'm your lawyer, Jimmy," Garrett reminded, "and I know better. And Reynolds knew better too."

"Yeah," said Jimmy Legg softly, "and you know better than to stick your beak where it don't belong. I'm dusting now, Garrett."

The lawyer grabbed him by the arm. "Hold it, Jimmy. Where are you going?"

"None of your business."

"What's got into you? The D.A. might make a stink because Reynolds didn't hold you. I may have to get in touch with you."

"You got my address."

"Don't take me for a child, Jimmy. You wouldn't go near your apartment till you were sure the police didn't want you again."

"I'll ring you at your office."

Howard Garrett shook his head slowly. "I don't like it."

Jimmy Legg laughed. It sounded like a glass cutter in action. "What's the beef?"

"Why," asked the attorney, "should a judge as scrupulously honest as Reynolds even think of letting you go scot free? Why do you refuse to tell me where you're holing in? Do you expect more trouble? And why did you come to me in the first place?"

"You know damned well why I come to you, Garrett."

The lawyer nodded. "Because I happen to own stock in Lansing Investment and you thought I could persuade them to go easy on you."

"So they went easy and I still don't get your beef."

"You're acting dumb, Jimmy. You know the Lansing people did nothing because I haven't even had a chance to talk to them. Still you got off—and I don't like it."

Jimmy Legg absently rearranged the silk handkerchief in the lawyer's breast pocket. "Everything's just ducky, Garrett."

"But—"

Jimmy Legg said, "Easy does it," and ambled off. He rounded the corner into Sunset and the instant he was out of his lawyer's sight his casual saunter became a rapid stride. His quick, purposeful steps faltered only when he looked behind to see if he was being tailed. But he saw no one and soon he gained a corner cut-rate drugstore.

He made for one of the phone booths at the far end, hunted in the directory, then dialed a number. The voice that responded said, "Hamilton Apartments," with an inflection calculated to let you know that the rents there were plenty high.

"Let's have Winnie Crawford." Jimmy Legg's voice sounded dry, almost frightened, and he had to repeat the name.

Another few moments and a languid contralto said: "Yes?"

"Are you alone, Winnie?"

There was a contralto gasp. "Jimmy! I thought they arrested you."

"I asked if you were alone."

"Yes." A moment's hesitation and she added: "Yes, darling."

"That's good. Now listen, honey," Legg said rapidly, "I'm coming up to your place. Pull the shades, lock the doors, and don't let anyone into your apartment till I get there."

"But I don't understand," said Winnie Crawford. "How did you get off? Did you get bail?"

"I'll tell you later, honey. I'm sitting on top of the world now and if you're smart there's a place right next to me for you. Get what I mean?"

"Of course, Jimmy. Only you'll have to give me a little time. You know I like you a lot but you mustn't rush—"

"That's good enough for me, sugar. You'll find out I like you enough for both of us when I get up there."

"But, Jimmy, maybe you shouldn't come up here. They'll see you at the desk downstairs."

"Don't worry, sugar. I'm coming up the back way."

Winnie Crawford said, "Good-bye, darling." She also said, "A fat chance you got to play bingo with me, you lousy bum," but Jimmy never heard that part for she had already cradled the receiver.

ONCE AGAIN JIMMY Legg consulted the directory. This time it was the yellow book and he searched under *Private Detectives* until he had his number, then dialed. The brittle, somewhat bored voice of a man answered.

"Is this Cellini Smith?" asked Jimmy Legg.

"Yes."

"Well, this is Jimmy Legg. I want to hire you to—"

"Listen, you underslung gunsel," interrupted Cellini Smith, "you couldn't hire me to laugh at you. Where'd you get the nickel to phone me?"

"It's on the level, Smith," protested Jimmy Legg. "I want you to do a job for me and I'm willing to give you a retainer."

"Get back under your damp rock, Legg. You couldn't retain a square meal, let alone retain me."

It never occurred to Jimmy Legg to get insulted. He said: "Look, Smith, there's real dough in this for you if you can help me out. I want you to come around and meet me."

"In the pig's eye," scoffed Cellini. "Whatever mess you're in, Legg, you probably deserve it."

"Now don't go off the deep end, Smith. You know your way around and you got to help me out. I'll pay in advance. I've got sugar on me right now."

There was a slight pause before Cellini Smith said: "That sounds better, crumb. How come you're out? I thought you were hooked on that Lansing Investment job?"

"That's just what I want to see you about, Smith. I want you to meet me at the Hamilton Apartments on Rossmore."

"Listen, you animated sewer, I'm not stepping out of this office till I find out what kind of a job you want me for—so you'd better tell me right now."

Jimmy Legg swore. "It's about that Lansing Investment job, Smith. I was in court this morning. The judge had me with my pants down but still he let me go. I want you to find out why that judge didn't hold me. Something stinks and I got to know."

"That sounds kind of interesting," said Cellini. "O.K. I don't promise to do anything, but I'll drop around for a look-see."

"Fine, Smith. The Hamilton Apartments in about forty minutes and make it the back entrance. If I ain't down there I'll have someone waiting to bring you up to the right apartment."

Cellini Smith promised to be there. Jimmy Legg pronged the receiver and left the booth. He went over to the counter and ordered a double-decker sandwich. Still eating the sandwich, he left the store and caught a Wilshire bus. After a while, he reached Rossmore, left the bus, and cut up the block toward a marble-fronted building.

When Jimmy Legg came abreast of the Hamilton Apartments, he paused to light a cigarette till the doorman's back was turned, then took the narrow alley on the north side. He walked down its length till he reached a fireproof door, pushed it open, and then stopped dead in his tracks.

Jimmy Legg's eyes bulged at what he saw and his Adam's apple bobbed up and down. His face was suddenly shiny with cold sweat. "No, no." His voice was almost a whisper. "Please don't."

Even as he spoke he knew his pleas were futile. There was a sharp report as a small-caliber gun went off and Jimmy Legg slowly tumbled forward—as if carefully choosing the spot of ground on which to die.

2

Rendezvous

CELLINI SMITH WORKED his feet back and forth, trying to get the sleep out of them. Finally, he yawned and stood up. He decided that he might as well get around and see what that Jimmy Legg business was about. Detectives who live in rent-due offices can't be choosy about clients.

Some twenty minutes later, Cellini turned off Wilshire at Rossmore and parked his heap of scrap iron opposite the Hamilton. He remembered that Legg had asked to meet him at the back entrance and he crossed the street and padded down the length of the alley on the north side—then stopped short. His face was a bored blank as he said: "Hello, Haenigson."

Ira Haenigson, detective-sergeant of Homicide, stood up from his examination of Jimmy Legg's corpse and made a wry face. "Why don't they draft you or something, Smith?"

"A killing?" asked Cellini disinterestedly. "Anyone I know?"

"Anyone you know!" The detective-sergeant seemed to swell like a blowfish. He turned to a porcine rookie. "Our friend wonders if it's anyone he knows."

The rookie laughed uncertainly.

"You're bloody well right it's someone you know!" Ira Haenigson suddenly shouted.

"How do you figure that?"

The Homicide man calmed himself, substituting irony for anger. "Now, I'm only a cop that goes out on homicide calls,

Smith. Just a dumb cop from Homicide. Do you understand?"

Cellini's brows furrowed as he gave the appearance of concentration. "You're a dumb cop from Homicide. I think I understand. Go on."

"That's right, Smith. And then I get a call to go out on a killing. Where is it? On Hollywood and Vine? On Wilshire and La Brea? Any place where it would be reasonable for you to show up? No indeed. The corpse is hidden in an alley by the rear door of an apartment building. Then by sheer coincidence you happen to show up in a place a quarter-hour later and you ask me if the body is anyone you know. Come, Smith, let me pinch your cheeks. You're so goddamned cute!"

The photographer finished taking his pictures of the body and chalk marks were made on the concrete outlining the position and angle at which it had fallen. Jimmy Legg was lifted on a stretcher and carted away. Then the fingerprint experts, sighing hopelessly as they regarded the stucco walls and the dull metal finish on the fireproof door, set about their jobs.

Cellini said: "I happened to be passing outside, Haenigson, when I noticed the department cars and I just came in here out of sheer curiosity to find out what had happened."

"Now that's entirely different, Smith. I shouldn't have left our cars on Rossmore right plunk in front of the apartment, eh?"

"I guess not."

"You great detective," said the detective-sergeant witheringly. "It so happens the department cars are not on Rossmore because I don't like to advertise my arrival. The cars are in *back* of this building. Anyone but a moron would have noticed that the body was just carried down the alley through to the street on the opposite side."

"That's what I meant," said Cellini smoothly. "I was passing through the other street and figured you were stopping at the Hamilton here so I came around the front—"

"All right," snapped the Homicide man. "Wrap it in Kleenex. Were you supposed to meet James Legg right here?"

Cellini Smith was a picture of innocence. "What's a Legg?"

"If you didn't show up here to meet Legg, then you came to meet his murderer. Which one was it?"

"I get it, Haenigson. Have I stopped beating my wife? Why don't you tell me what this is all about?" Cellini demanded.

"James Legg muscled his way out of court on a burglary rap this morning. An hour later he's garbage. A two-bit homicide, Smith, but the kind that makes good headlines. Can the underworld make a mockery out of our courts? Get what I'm driving at?"

"Sure," nodded Cellini. "If you don't crack it quick you need somebody to throw to the wolves—and I'm handy."

"Exactly, Smith. This happens to be the wrong kind of case to play button-button with the police. So you better open up and say what you're doing here and who you were supposed to meet."

"I was driving by and saw the department cars," began Cellini, "and I figured I'd see what was cooking—"

Ira Haenigson's bulky figure slowly advanced on Cellini. "Get out! Quick!" Cellini didn't move. Other than a narrowing of the eyes, his face was infuriatingly calm. But the tapered body was braced with catlike tensity to meet the Homicide man's elephantine rush.

Haenigson suddenly thought better of it and halted. "That's better," said Cellini, "—and safer." He wheeled and walked out.

CELLINI SMITH SAT in his parked car debating with himself. His client had been murdered. It would be little better than sucker stuff to try and nail the killer out of charity. Besides, whoever mayhemmed Jimmy Legg didn't do mankind any disservice. But there was Ira Haenigson and his threat could not be regarded idly. He could make much of Cellini's appearance at the scene shortly after the murder—and he would certainly refuse to accept the true explanation for it. Haenigson would never believe that a gunsel of Legg's caliber would hire a peeper.

Cellini sighed and got out of the car. He had no alternative but to follow through—and to do so before Haenigson began wondering what Legg was doing in these parts.

He passed through the palm-studded doorway of the Hamilton and approached the desk. He asked: "Does Mr. James Legg live here?"

The clerk, a delicate, lavender specimen, flipped through his files. "Now let me see. That should be under *L*. No, sir, I'm sorry. I've never heard of Mr. Legg."

"You've heard, all right. That's the guy who was shot outside in your alley an hour ago."

"Oh, you know of it?" said the clerk brightly. "I'm so glad. I'm such a poor liar."

"Fine. But did Legg have an apartment here?"

"Certainly not." The clerk sounded offended. "We don't lease apartments to such rowdies—such, such potential corpses."

Cellini leaned over the desk. "Listen, my androgynous friend. If Legg didn't park his shoes here then he visited somebody and the chances are you know who it is. Now why don't you open up and dish out an intelligible remark?"

"Fine, sir! I'm glad you asked that because we like to bruit about the idea that we supply no information about our lessees. And it's no use glowering because I know you're not from the police and I simply refuse to be intimidated by—"

Cellini didn't trust himself to linger longer. He walked out and circled around to the alley where Jimmy Legg had met, in rapid succession, his destroyer and his Maker. Haenigson hadn't even bothered to post a cop. Murderers, he well knew, rarely return to the scene of their crime.

Cellini passed by the tradesmen's entrance and pushed through a smaller door beyond. He found himself in the cellar. The janitor, a grimy individual in overalls, was laying out a game of solitaire on a side-turned wardrobe trunk.

Cellini dropped a dollar bill on the trunk. "I'll bet you that buck you don't know how many cards there are in that deck."

"Fifty-two," said the surprised janitor.

"It's yours. Now, what do you know about Jimmy Legg?"

The janitor palmed the greenback. "For a moment I thought you was Santa Claus. Well, all I know is some dame found this Legg guy and started screaming like she lost her virtue so I run outside and called the cops. That's all."

"Didn't you hear any shots some time before that?"

"So a car backfired," said the janitor. "So what? That's like I asked the cops. I asked am I expected to go about having premonitions about a murder?"

"And you never saw or heard of Jimmy Legg before?"

"Nope. Not even for a sawbuck."

"Well, he must have been visiting somebody here and I've got to get a line on it. Start telling me about the tenants."

"We got five floors and six big apartments on each," began

the janitor. "In 1-A we got a nice old couple. They're vegetari-ans. Next to them in 2-A is a family that's vacationing. Then—"

"Forget that. No families. Legg must have been visiting a dame or a man. What single tenants are there?"

"Only three because the apartments are pretty expensive for one guy. In 2-D we got an old maid."

"No good. Next."

"Then there's a guy with a Vandyke beard in 4-C. He owns a few oil wells and he hides under his bed all day and drinks."

"No good. Who's the other?"

"A blonde that's something. Her body ain't ersatz either. She's strictly the wrong side of the tracks but you got to have sugar to live here so I guess she's got it."

"That's a good bet," said Cellini eagerly. "What's her name?"

"Winnie Crawford in 4-E."

"Who's keeping her?"

"This'll kill you—nobody!"

"Are you sure?"

"So help me. She don't like men and it's sure a waste because if I ever seen production for use, she's it. It's ridiculous!" The janitor sounded offended.

"It's impossible," said Cellini, "and I'll check right now."

CELLINI LEANED ON the button and heard the chimes sounding inside of 4-E. A husky contralto yelled: "Relax. I'm not deaf."

A moment later the door was opened by a woman in her late twenties and Cellini could see what the janitor had meant. She was something that the Hayes office would have banned even in a burlap bag. At the moment, however, she wore a form-clinging, silk dress that would have caught male eyes in a nudist colony.

"Who asked for you?" Her hands rested aggressively on her hips and she seemed surprised to see him.

"Are you Winnie Crawford?" Cellini asked.

"Uh-huh. Spring it."

"It's about Jimmy Legg. He's not coming."

"Why not?"

Cellini grinned. This was the right party. He walked by her through a short foyer and found himself in the living-room. He wondered if there was anyone else around and toured through kitchen, dinette, bedroom, bath, and dressing alcove but drew a blank. He returned to the living-room to find Winnie Crawford leveling a huge revolver at him with both hands.

Cellini sighted some bourbon on an end table and poured himself a stiff drink. He said: "That thing you got in your soft, white, creamy hands. You'd better put it down."

"What's the idea smelling around this place?" she countered. "What are you looking for?"

Cellini tasted the drink. It was good liquor. "I was just wondering if you were alone, Winnie—whether you had a couple of boy friends in the Frigidaire or something."

"I got no boy friends and I'm alone and I can take care of myself. You better tell me what you want. Make it quick."

"And you'd better ditch that rod," said Cellini casually, "if it happens to be the one that killed Jimmy Legg this morning."

Winnie Crawford sat down heavily on a divan. Cellini gave silent approval of the exposed legs. He walked over, removed the revolver from her unresisting fingers, and broke it. It was fully loaded and didn't smell as if it had been recently fired.

He tossed the revolver aside, half-filled a glass with straight bourbon, and handed it to her. Her face was white and drawn and her fingers trembled. He decided that Jimmy Legg must have meant a lot to her.

She drank deeply and seemed to regain control of herself. "I never got anything but trouble from that chiseling heel," she muttered.

Cellini decided, on second thought, that Jimmy Legg meant nothing to her and that she was worried about her own skin. "Did you kill him?" he asked.

She registered a look of disgust and pulled her skirts over her knees. She was her normal self again. "Where did it happen?"

"Downstairs in the alley at the side of this building. He was sneaking up the back way to see you."

"What gives you the ridiculously fantastic idea that he was visiting me?" Her head went back and the nose up in what she hoped was a chilling, regal look.

He grinned. "Too late to backwater now, Winnie. Get down to the monosyllables. You're more at home there."

She regarded him speculatively for a moment, then sighed resignedly. "All right. Tell me about it and especially what your racket is."

"My handle is Cellini Smith and I'm a private op. Legg phoned me to meet him in the back alley but when I got there he wasn't receiving. So I *cherchez-ed* the dame and here I am."

"What did he want you for?"

Cellini shrugged. "Something about the cops and a safe-cracking job. At the Lansing Investment Company, I think it was."

"I know all that. How come they didn't hold him?"

"That's exactly what Mr. Legg wanted me to find out."

"Oh. Listen, Smith, you know I didn't kill Jimmy. I'm just not the type."

"Perish the thought," he said. "Go on."

"BUT I GOT other reasons for wanting to be kept out of this mess," Winnie Crawford continued. "Good reasons. Get out of here, Smith, and just forget all about me."

"Not a chance. The shams are down on me because they think I know more than I do and I'm not the kind of hero that'll get in a mess to save the name of some fair twist. Besides, Winnie, you forget the cops'll get around to you just as easily as I did."

"I guess that's so," she admitted. She drained her glass and nervously poured more bourbon.

"Of course it's so. Loosen up, Winnie, and tell me what you know about all this."

"Nothing. Jimmy phoned that he was coming up here. That's all. I was surprised, too, they let him go."

"Why was Jimmy Legg coming here? This is a pretty classy place you've got—not the kind of thing Legg could afford."

She drew herself up. "I beg your pardon?"

"Oh, come off it, Winnie. You know as well as I do that you look like a love captive in a penthouse."

"Get this, you louse! I'm nobody's keptie. Just because I'm beautiful and there ain't no cockroaches in the kitchen is no sign I am."

"All right. Simmer down. Your dimples disappear when you get angry. If you're not doing light housekeeping for a male, then who pays for all this?"

"Men," pronounced Winnie Crawford, "are beasts."

"Sure—the cads—but Jimmy Legg was still liquidated right outside this building," he reminded her, "and the cops will be here in a little while."

"I'm not worried about the cops. I was up here all the time and it's no crime if Jimmy was visiting me."

"That kind of weasel talk doesn't jell," he hammered. "I've got to get some kind of lead on this and I think you can supply it. So come across."

She chewed at one of her long, vermilion nails. "Listen, could you tell me why Jimmy was killed?"

"Holy mother of hell!" he exploded. "What do you think I'm trying to find out?"

"Well, when you do find out you'll tell me, won't you?"

"Sure and I'll pass out a ten dollar bill with each syllable," he replied not too subtly.

She stood up and walked over to a corner taboret that served as the bar. She opened a cocktail shaker and removed a fat roll of bills. Carefully, she counted five wrinkled twenty dollar bills into his hand. "Here. I'm hiring you to find out why Jimmy was killed."

"*Why* he was killed? Don't you want to know *who* killed him?"

"That's not so important."

"And suppose I pin it on you?"

"I'll take the chance."

He slipped the money into his slender wallet, frowning. "And I'll take the job, Winnie, though you're a rather phoney client. Are you sure you and Jimmy weren't soulmates?"

"You heard me. Why do men always think of only one thing?"

"I remember—because they're beasts. But you're not Bryn Mawr stock, Winnie, and you weren't born with any gold shovel in your mouth. Someone's paying your bills. Who?"

"Why can't you get it through your head I'm nobody's woman? I spent my life shining up to slick chiselers and visiting firemen. Now I'm through with the whole lousy breed and I'm relaxing."

Her voice was hard and grating and carried conviction. Cellini surrendered the point. "All right, you're stainless. Then where did you get that fat roll of kohl-rabi you flashed before and how do you pay the rent here?"

"That's none of your business. Just go and find out why Jimmy was killed."

"What difference does it make to you? Why was he coming up here anyway?"

"Nothing doing."

"Then at least tell me what time Jimmy Legg phoned to say he was coming."

"Around eleven."

"That's about when he phoned me," said Cellini. "All right. When the cops get around to you just tell them I'm handling your interests and they'll put you under arrest immediately."

3

Careless Lead

CELLINI SMITH STEPPED into the hallway, shutting the door to Winnie Crawford's apartment behind him, just as the elevator pulled level with the floor and a huge man stepped out.

Cellini said: "Hello, Mack. No, I'm not betting."

Mack was square and solid as the truck he was named after. There was a lot of him and his customers never fooled with him for he was one of the town's toughest bookmakers. But they liked him. "Your loss," he replied. "Everybody's taking me. Say, don't tell me you just came out of Winnie's stable. Please don't tell me that."

"Why not?"

"Because then I'd have to beat you to a gooey pulp, Cellini, and I hate to beat friends to gooey pulps."

Cellini looked up at the big man and smiled crookedly. "Maybe," he said, "but I never fight Queensberry with monsters like you. But I don't get it—why should you jump me for coming out of Winnie Crawford's apartment?"

"Because I long ago decided that if I can't have her then nobody else will."

"You can relax. That type's a little too synthetic for my tastes."

"You just don't know her, Cellini. She's the laziest white woman in the country without hookworm—but what a build!"

"You beast," said Cellini. "How come she snaps her fingers at a great big he-man like you?"

"Now you'd think Winnie would know better, wouldn't you?" His voice was charged with complaint. "That double-dealing twist gets her mitts on some real dough and right away she's through with men."

"Where'd she get the dough?"

"I wish I knew. I keep asking her but she don't even bother to lie. It's a hell of a life."

"She might have gotten it from her family," suggested Cellini. "Heiress stuff—like in the movies."

Mack's laughter sounded like the fall of bowling pins. "Her family is the backbone of the W.P.A., when it's sober, and she was a carhop in a drive-in."

"Then how'd she get out of it?"

"A small-time crook saw her and picked her up. Maybe you know him. Jimmy Legg."

"Go on." Cellini hoped his voice was casual.

"So she stayed with him for a while. Jimmy Legg played the horses through me so I happened to meet Winnie. Then I took over and we made it a twosome until I made a big mistake."

"What was that?"

"I figured to keep her out of trouble while I was working so I got her a job with one of my customers. Switchboard girl at the Lansing Investment Company."

Cellini took a deep breath. At last something was beginning to connect. "Then what, Mack?"

"Then she left me flat and moved in with the head of that place—Lansing himself. Lansing is a big bettor with me so I didn't even have the satisfaction of beating him up. Then a few months later Winnie got this dough somehow and she ditched all of us."

"All this is very interesting."

"Winnie ain't interesting," said Mack. "This no-man business of hers is just irritating. There should be a law."

"I mean Jimmy Legg. He cracked the safe at this same Lansing Investment a few days ago."

"Yeah," frowned the big man. "I heard. But I don't catch."

"And that's not all," said Cellini slowly. "I was seeing Winnie Crawford before to get me a client and to let her know that Jimmy Legg was killed this morning."

The violence of the explosion was unexpected. For a full two minutes, colorful expletives issued from Mack's big mouth and bounced through the hallway of the Hamilton Apartments.

"Why the excitement?" Cellini was finally able to ask.

"Excitement! That guy Legg has been backing platers with me for the last year. *On credit!* I got over eight hundred bucks in I.O.U.s from him."

"Well, you can't collect now."

"Say, nobody runs out on Mack. Not even a corpse. I'll get it if—" He suddenly paused. "Where's your angle in the killing?" he asked quietly.

Cellini shrugged. "Strictly the dough in it."

Mack's two large hands vised Cellini's shoulders. "Say, I don't like the way you were leading me on before."

"Your paws, Mack. I'm asking you only once. Drop them." Cellini stared fixedly at the big man's tie-pin.

The hands slowly loosened their grip. "Hell, Cellini, we're friends. We don't want to fight. There's a nag called Inquisitor running at Holly Park today. That should be a good hunch for a dick like you."

"Some other time." Cellini made for the elevator.

CELLINI SMITH WENT through every afternoon paper, reading the sensationalized accounts of how one Manny Simms had hidden under Judge Reynolds' desk, forcing the jurist to release Jimmy Legg.

It puzzled him. Obviously, Jimmy Legg had neither instigated Manny Simms' enterprise nor had he been aware of it—else he would not have wanted to hire Cellini to discover the cause of his release. This Manny Simms had acted either on his own or for someone else—but why? Why should Simms accept the certainty of a couple of years in jail to spring Jimmy Legg? Perhaps Howard Garrett, Legg's mouthpiece, had the answer.

Cellini turned his coupé around and urged it back to Hollywood. A half-hour later, he pushed by a frosted glass door in the Equitable Building that read: *Howard Garrett—Attorney at Law.* Under it were the names of a couple of junior partners.

The black-haired, eagle-beaked secretary-receptionist released the fetching smile reserved for men only and asked if she could help. Her voice had the high, irritating whine of a sawmill.

Cellini blocked the smile with a come-on leer. Secretaries can be useful. "I'm a very important guy," he said, "and I want to hold converse with Mr. Garrett about a crumb—one Jimmy Legg."

The secretary giggled, plugged in the switchboard, and announced him with that voice. He passed into an inner office and sank into a leather chair beside the desk. Howard Garrett, with a lawyer's caution, waited for him to speak first.

Flatly, without frills, Cellini explained who he was and what he wanted. When he was finished, Garrett said: "I'd like to help but I couldn't give even the police any information of value."

"I don't get it," insisted Cellini. "Don't tell me you didn't know that Jimmy Legg was probably guilty of cracking the Lansing Investment safe."

"We're both men of the world, Mr. Smith, and so I don't mind admitting, off the record, that I knew Legg was guilty. But even the guilty have the right to counsel."

"Sure—if they can pay for it. But if you knew Legg was guilty, weren't you surprised when Reynolds let him off?"

"Naturally. Surprised, and pleased because my client had won."

"Did you get Manny Simms to pull that trick of threatening the judge from under the desk?"

"No. I didn't know of it. I don't even know this Simms individual, and I don't know who later killed James Legg."

The lawyer was unruffled, even slightly amused. A smooth article, Cellini thought. He asked: "What happened after Legg and you went out of the courtroom?"

"Nothing. He simply left me in front of the Hall of Justice and we went our separate ways."

Cellini lit a cigarette and thoughtfully watched the smoke curl up. "I just remembered," he said abruptly, "I know a guy who was pinched for stealing a bottle of milk. He's broke and I wonder if you could give him a break and try to spring him."

"I'm sorry, Mr. Smith, but attorneys eat like everyone else and I can't afford charity cases."

"That's what I thought," snapped Cellini. "Yet you take on a nickel-mooching gunsel like Jimmy Legg. How come?"

"I don't understand, Mr. Smith."

"Where did Legg get the retainer to hire you? It certainly wasn't from any dough he stole from Lansing because you're too smart to stick your neck out like that. Why did you defend him?"

Howard Garrett stood up. "I don't understand your tricky antagonism toward me, Mr. Smith, and I certainly don't have to stand for it. I'm sorry I can't say I'm glad I met you."

Cellini left little doubt that the feeling was mutual and walked out, closing the door. He leaned over the secretary-receptionist's desk. "How about giving me Jimmy Legg's home address?"

"Have you asked Mr. Garrett?"

"Why ask him when I can have the pleasure of asking you?"

She giggled and reached for a box of filing cards. The leer was paying off. She supplied an address in her sawmill voice and added philosophically: "Isn't it just awful how the world is full of murder and sorrow, like this poor Mr. Legg?"

"Legg was no awful loss and he wasn't very poor. He probably stole a batch of bills from the Lansing Investment—crisp bills as shiny as your hair—and they're probably waiting to be found someplace right now."

The giggle sounded again. "My hair's shiny only because I haven't washed it in a long time. Isn't it funny? But it's peculiar how Mr. Garrett defended Mr. Legg in this Lansing burglary charge even though he owns a lot of stock in the Lansing company."

The strident-voiced secretary went on to say how she wasn't doing anything that night, but Cellini wasn't listening. He had hold of something good—a mouthpiece representing a burglar who had robbed a firm in which he was a heavy stockholder.

CELLINI SMITH FISHED among the tools under the

seat of his car and selected a heavy screwdriver. It would be as good a jimmy for forcing a door as anything else.

The apartment building where the late Jimmy Legg had parked his hat was a dreary affair with dark halls that smelled of unappetizing cooking. Cellini walked up to the third floor, then down the hall, checking the name-plates, till he had the one he wanted.

He was glad to find the door a weak-looking affair. He inserted the screwdriver into the crack between lock and jamb, and the door suddenly sprang back inside. It had not been locked.

Puzzled, he stepped over the threshold. From the corner of one eye he thought he detected a movement and tried to duck but was too late. He felt himself yanked backward with one powerful jerk and a telegraph pole seemed to wind around his neck. It was unexpected and very efficient. The pole around Cellini's neck was an arm and his assailant's other arm circled his ribs with the same bone-crushing effect.

Cellini tried to twist around to get at his attacker but he was no match for those powerful arms. He kicked back and up at the groin with the heel of his shoe but connected with nothing. The other was an old hand at such tricks.

The arm around Cellini's neck tightened and he was slowly forced down till his back was in a painful arch. His breath became short and constricted. His fists clenched from the pain and he slowly became aware of the screwdriver still in his hand. He reversed it so that the point faced his attacker and drove it back, with all his power, in a short, vicious arc. There was a muffled yell of pain and the encircling arms dropped away from Cellini. He whirled—to find himself facing Mack's mammoth figure.

Astonishment mingled with the pain in Mack's face when he saw Cellini. He mumbled something indistinguishable and pulled his shirt up to examine the wound made in his side by the screwdriver. Though deep, the cut was small and narrow and the blood came only in a reluctant trickle. He took his undershirt off and tied it tightly around his body, binding the wound. Then he dressed again and suddenly became voluble.

"I know it looks bad jumping you like that, Cellini, but I swear I thought it was someone else. I wouldn't—"

"Who did you think I was?"

"Manny Simms. The guy that sprang Jimmy Legg out of court this morning."

"That's not good enough, Mack. Try again." Cellini's voice was not threatening but he kept one hand in his pocket over a small, .25 caliber automatic and the bookie suddenly broke into a sweat.

"I mean it," he insisted. "I know Manny Simms and I tell you I saw him downstairs. I thought it was him coming after me. I'll show you."

They walked over to a window and Mack pointed down at a black sedan on the other side of the street. Two men stood by it and they seemed to be staring at the very window where they were. "That's them. The one on the left is Simms. If you was close enough you'd spot the toothpick in his puss. Always has one."

CELLINI RELAXED. "O.K. I didn't think Simms would be out on bail this quick. Who's the other guy with him?"

Mack shrugged. "Another torpedo. Birds of a feather. If you

want to go after them to make up a bridge foursome I'll help you."

"Not right now. I'd first like to find out who killed Legg and it wasn't Manny Simms because he was under the judge's apron at the time. But let's hear what *you're* doing here."

"Hell, man, you know Jimmy Legg stuck me for eight hundred dollars. And when you told me he was fogged I started figuring that maybe the dough he stole from the Lansing outfit was up here, and I could kind of collect the debt on my own."

"How did you get in here without breaking the lock?"

Unexpectedly, Mack grinned. His voice was a conflict of modesty and bragging as he confessed: "You don't know it, man, but I was the smoothest thing in the safe-cracking line in my youth and it takes a good lock to stop me."

Cellini looked at him sharply but he seemed sincere. "How come you stayed out of college?"

"I was smart. When I become too big to be inconspicuous I just quit and become a bookie. I had a terrific technique, too, for those days."

"All right, you're wonderful. Let's look around for that Lansing dough."

It was a small, three-room apartment, sparsely furnished, and there weren't many likely hiding places. With a fine disregard for the furnishings, Mack took a jackknife from his pocket, and began slashing open cushions, pillows and bed mattress.

Cellini checked through closets and cupboards, searched under rugs and behind pictures, pawed through drawers, and even sounded walls. There was nothing even remotely suggesting the Lansing Investment loot. The only item of interest was a small cache of tools he came upon in the icebox. It contained hammer, nails, a spool of wire, pliers, and some files. It was, decided Cellini, a very sorry-looking burglar's kit.

He remembered that people often rolled money into shades and walked over to a window in time to hear the squeal of brakes as a car came to a halt in the street below. There was familiar authority about that squeal and Cellini looked down. Detective-sergeant Ira Haenigson and a couple of his men were getting out of the car below. Across the way, Manny Simms and his fellow hood climbed into their black sedan and decided to mosey along.

Cellini said: "We weren't the only ones with the bright idea of casing this place. The minions of the law are here."

"Let 'em come," replied the disgusted bookmaker. "They'll only find magnolia."

Cellini went into the kitchen and looked out the back window. It was just an empty lot below. He returned to the living-room. "No fire escape."

"It's all right. There's a back way."

They went out, proceeded down the end of the hallway, and started down the back stairs as they heard the Homicide men come up the opposite way. They reached the street and saw no sign of Manny Simms.

"I could use a drink," declared Mack. "Let's try the Greek's."

Cellini agreed and a couple of minutes later they pulled up in front of a hole-in-wall honky-tonk.

They stepped out of the coupé and started inside when Cellini heard the sudden acceleration of a supercharged engine. He whirled in time to see a black sedan charging down the block toward them. Automatically, he wedged a foot between Mack's ankles, bringing the big man crashing to the ground, and, in the same instant, threw himself prone.

It was only split seconds before the sedan was by them and dime-turning the next corner. But in that time there was a crashing, trip-hammer *rat-a-tat* that made it seem very long, a vicious spatter of bullets that seemed never to stop. The counterpoint of a woman's hysterical scream, the hoarse shout of a passing motorist, the running, panicky feet that wanted only to get far away—all made the moments seem that much longer.

And when Cellini and Mack finally stood up they could see a strip of small holes against the building that housed the Greek's saloon. The strip was at a height of some forty inches. If they had been standing up the bullets from Manny Simms' sub-machine gun would have flattened out inside their stomachs.

"Shades of Capone," said Cellini unsteadily.

4

Wild Goose

THE GREEK, A bulbous-nosed, stocky man, shoved two more glasses of suspect Scotch over the bar to Mack and Cellini Smith. "That kind shootings is beeg time," he said. He patted an obsolete and rusty .455 Webley revolver on the liquor case. "But next time they shoot bullets into my building I geeve them with this."

"I'll geeve that —— Manny Simms the lumps," said Mack darkly. He and Cellini were both several sheets to windward, their anger over serving as targets for Simms increasing with each drink.

Cellini tapped the bar for emphasis. "There can be only one explanation why he's gunning for us."

"He only needs one," Mack pointed out.

"He saw us go into Jimmy Legg's apartment and there must be something there that Simms was afraid we'd see or get our hands on."

"The haul from the Lansing job," guessed Mack.

"I wouldn't be so sure. That doesn't explain why Simms held up the judge to get Legg off. He would have let Jimmy go to jail and then gotten the loot for himself."

"I geeve them shootings," said the one-tracked Greek.

"Furthermore," Cellini persisted, "if it's just for the dough that Legg stole, then Manny Simms would be trying to get it from us—not just kill us."

"All right," hiccupped the overgrown bookie, "so you explain me why I got to go around ducking Thompson subs."

"I wish I knew."

The Greek said hopefully: "Thees people who do the shootings—maybe they are Eyetalian."

Cellini drained his glass. "We had plenty time to go through Jimmy Legg's apartment before Haenigson got there and we found nothing out of the ordinary—excepting what's in the icebox."

"What about it?"

"That's where Legg hid the tools of his trade."

"Such as?" asked Mack interestedly.

"Pliers, wire, nails, and stuff."

"That Legg was small-time," declared Mack professionally. "All I ever needed to clean a box was a fine sewing needle. But

From the black sedan charging past came a vicious spatter of bullets.

it still don't explain why Simms got Homicidal about us."

The Greek refilled their glasses with the dubious Scotch. Cellini snapped his fingers as a thought crossed his mind. "Say, do you think my luscious client is in back of this?"

"I love Winnie madly but I got to admit there's nothing that slut ain't capable of."

"Let's see." Cellini went to the wall phone and dialed the Hamilton Apartments. When he heard Winnie Crawford's voice he said: "A hundred-buck retainer doesn't give you the right to try and get me chopped down."

"What are you talking about? You sound drunk."

"That's only from the liquor in me and I'm talking about Manny Simms. Is he the guy who pays your bills?"

"Damn you!" Winnie Crawford exploded. "I told you I was alone and liking it. Cut out the sex stuff."

"O.K., Winnie. Simmer down. Do you know Manny Simms?"

"I never heard of the guy."

The throaty voice was hesitant and falsely casual. Cellini knew she was lying. She said: "Listen, I gave you a century to find out why Jimmy was killed. What about it?"

"Give me time, Winnie. I'm lousy with clues."

He pronged the receiver and returned unsteadily to the bar for another drink.

"What'd she say?" asked Mack.

"Nothing much. She blew her own strumpet about males and claimed she never heard of Manny Simms when I know damned well she read all about him in the papers."

"I love her," Mack sighed. "It'd be funny if she killed Legg."

Cellini finished his drink. "Haenigson's probably still messing around Legg's place. I'll go see what he knows about Simms."

"And I'll see if I can pick up Simms," declared the bookie.

Cellini shook his head. "You wait here for me. I want to be around when we catch up with Manny Simms."

CELLINI SMITH'S HEAD was somewhat clearer and his step steadier by the time he got back to Jimmy Legg's apartment. He pushed open the door to find the police still at it. Two of them were taking apart the plumbing in the hope of finding some tell-tale residue in the U-traps, another was dusting for prints, and yet another was tape-measuring the rooms to make sure they had missed no hiding place. Ira Haenigson was doing a thorough job.

The detective-sergeant himself sat on the ripped living-room sofa, supervising the proceedings. He fish-eyed Cellini. "I know," he said. "You were passing by downstairs and you saw the squad car."

"No. I knew you were here and I wanted to talk to you."

"Sure you knew, because"—Haenigson's voice became milder—"you took this place apart before we got here."

"Me?" Cellini was injured innocence.

"No one else. And so help me, Smith, if it really was you, you'll be eating San Quentin plum pudding next Christmas."

"Why pick on me? Why couldn't Manny Simms have searched this place before you got here?"

"What about Manny Simms?"

Cellini could see that the Homicide man was interested and followed up his advantage. "I'm here for an armistice, Haenigson. You stop treating me like a dishrag and I'll open up."

"It's a deal," said the detective-sergeant after a moment's hesitation. "If you're really on the level. Let's hear."

"Fine. I went to the alley behind the Hamilton to meet Jimmy Legg there. He wanted me to find out why he wasn't held in court this morning."

"He didn't put Simms up to that job of springing him?"

"That's what it looks like. After you and I had our sweet parting I checked and found that Legg was going to the Hamilton to meet a dame. But I suppose you found that out."

Ira Haenigson nodded. "That Winnie Crawford tramp. I don't know what to make of her. She looks faster than Legg's speed."

"I'm wondering myself. Anyway, she hired me on the killing and I came around here about an hour ago with a friend of mine. Just then I saw you pull up so I didn't come in."

"You sure of that, Smith?"

"Honest Injun. I went away for a drink and when I got out of the car along comes this Manny Simms and tries to chop me down with a Thompson sub."

Cellini wasn't sure whether the Homicide man's frown indicated perplexity or disappointment over Manny Simm's failure. He asked: "How come Simms is loose for such sport? Why wasn't he held?"

"Good lawyer, small bail," shrugged Haenigson. "He didn't commit any homicide—just threats—and there wasn't even any bullets in the rod he pulled on the judge so he got out on low bail. But what do you want me to do about it, Smith?"

"I want you to help me find Manny Simms. I don't like the idea of that baby gunning for me."

"Sure, Smith. I wouldn't mind finding out for myself why he's wasting bullets on you. What do you think?"

"I don't know. My hunch is that it's tied up with the dough that Jimmy Legg souped out of the Lansing Investment safe."

"He didn't steal any dough from them."

Cellini stared at Haenigson. "I don't get it. What then did he steal from that safe?"

"That's what I'd like to find out, Smith. That's why I'm up here taking this place apart right now."

"Didn't Lansing Investment make any claims about stolen stuff?"

"Nothing at all. They just asked us to forget the whole thing. Mr. Lansing seemed to think his firm would get a bad reputation if the public found out it was successfully burgled."

"But if Lansing didn't charge Jimmy Legg with anything

then why was he arrested and brought into court this morning?"

"They couldn't very well avoid it because Legg also slugged the janitor and a secretary and they identified him."

"Say," asked Cellini, "do you think this Lansing Investment is a crooked outfit?"

"Could be," said Ira Haenigson. "Could be."

CELLINI SMITH GOT out of the elevator and entered the offices of the Lansing Investment Company. The place was large with lots of pale-faced stenographers and sleek-haired clerks who gave their investment spiels with all the fervor of a Fuller brush man.

Cellini asked to see Mr. Lansing himself. He told what it was about, gave his pedigree, showed identification, and when he refused to settle for a vice-president he was finally shown past the balustrade and into an ornate inner office.

Mr. Lansing was bluff, confident, and obviously never tortured by self-doubt. Stocky from good feeding rather than hard work, he was in his forties and had a golf-tan complexion.

"Deplorable this murder of James Legg, very deplorable," declared the president of Lansing Investment without preamble. "Death except from God or the legal executioner has always shocked me."

"It's very cruel," said Cellini.

"Yes, quite. Of course you realize, Mr. Smith, that the murder of James Legg and his lamentable burglary of our offices is sheer coincidence and can have no conceivable connection."

"If I realized that," replied Cellini, "I wouldn't be here."

"My good man, do you imply that we may have a connection—even a remote one—with murder?"

"Perhaps not so remote."

Mr. Lansing blinked. His voice was sharp. "Sir, my wife always kills a good joke but my connection with homicide ends there. It's been a pleasure." He stood up.

Cellini didn't budge. "Is your wife a luscious blonde?" he asked innocently.

"I don't understand you, Mr. Smith, and I don't wish to. I'm afraid I can waste no more time."

Cellini snapped his fingers. "How stupid of me! Of course your wife isn't a blonde. I was confusing her with Winnie Crawford."

Lansing stopped in his tracks. He sat down again with a sickly smile, hauling forth brandy bottle and glasses from the desk. Cellini helped himself, then reached into the cigar humidor. He wondered if the investment manipulator had a solid alibi for the murder time.

Lansing finally broke the silence. "Mr. Smith, you don't seem the prudish sort so you probably understand the necessity for an occasional peccadillo to relieve marital boredom."

"Sure. Especially peccadillos built like Winnie."

"Quite, sir, quite. And I'm sorry that you and I got off on the wrong foot."

"You mean the wrong Legg."

Lansing tried a laugh and missed. "It's just my natural desire to prevent any unsavory talk of murders and robberies in connection with Lansing Investment. Our business depends so much on public confidence."

"Then why don't you help me so that I might clear it up?" Cellini suggested.

"By all means," said Lansing with forced eagerness. "Only there's very little I can tell you."

CELLINI SMITH SAID: "Start with the reason why you people didn't press any charge against Jimmy Legg when he knocked over the safe in this place."

"That was only because we'd much rather absorb a small loss than have such bad publicity," replied Lansing.

"What did the small loss amount to?"

"Oh, nothing of importance really."

"Was it money? Did you have currency in the safe?"

"I don't think so," said Lansing evasively. "Just some non-negotiable bonds, I believe."

"Aren't you sure?"

"I happened to be out of town the day of the robbery, Mr. Smith, and I haven't had a chance to check. However, I'll do so and mail you a list of the items."

"That's a lie," said Cellini deliberately. "You know damned well what was stolen."

Lansing squeezed another smile out of his face. "Please allow a difference of opinion, Mr. Smith."

Cellini sampled the brandy again and got up to leave. Apprehensively, Lansing asked: "Mr. Smith, can I rely on your discretion about that Winnie Crawford—um—involvement?"

"Yes. How come you two broke it up though?"

"You know how it is about these affairs of the heart, Mr. Smith. One or the other cools."

"How did you happen to meet her?"

"She used to work here as my secretary."

"And your checkbook said, 'I love you.' Which still doesn't

explain where Winnie gets her dough if you're not around anymore."

"I'm afraid I don't understand you, Mr. Smith."

"There's no need to." Cellini started out and Lansing took his arm in a brotherly fashion, telling him to drop around if he ever wished some real good investment tips. They passed into the outer office and Cellini noted a large safe built into one of the corners. "Is that the one Legg cracked?" he asked.

"Yes, Mr. Smith."

"I thought the door was blown off."

"Of course, but the safe manufacturers have been in since. They put on new hinges and repaired it."

"All right." Cellini walked out, past the balustrade, into the reception-room. Waiting in one of the club chairs was Howard Garrett, Jimmy Legg's mouthpiece in court that morning.

"Surprise," said Cellini. "Are you here to return what your dead client stole—or to split the loot with Lansing?"

Garrett examined his fingernails, studied the ceiling, and gave no indication that he had heard. Cellini shrugged and walked out of the Lansing Investment offices.

A stout woman worked a vacuum cleaner over the carpeting of the hallway. Cellini could see her key-ring, hanging from the keyhole of a broom closet farther down the hallway. As he passed by the closet, his hand reached out and silently and quickly transferred the ring of keys to his own pocket.

CELLINI SMITH PHONED Ira Haenigson and asked if they had located Manny Simms and his Tommy. They had not and he returned to his car and headed for the Greek's gin-joint to get Mack.

The gargantuan bookie took his liquor well. With another eight or nine drinks fermenting in him, his neck was redder and his voice hoarser but he showed little other effect.

Cellini straddled a stool and poured for himself. The bookie asked what was cooking. "I just checked with Haenigson," Cellini replied. "They haven't caught up with Simms yet."

"That's good," said Mack. "Simms is our meat. What else you been doing?"

"I dropped up to see one of your customers—the president of Lansing Investment."

"What's he got to say?"

"He called my client a peccadillo and he showed me the safe that Jimmy Legg cracked."

"What about it?"

"Plenty," said Cellini. "Legg never touched that safe. The manufacturers were supposed to have put on new hinges but the ones I saw there aren't new."

"That's a laugh. We go nimrodding through Legg's dump looking for the stuff he stole and then you find out that he never even cleaned the Lansing safe."

"I didn't say that."

Mack stared accusingly at his drink. "I don't catch."

"I just said that our defunct friend didn't crack the safe Mr. Lansing showed me."

"Oh. I see it all now, Cellini. Like hell!"

The Greek said, "Thees shootings and the drinks are bad combination," and left to service a couple at a back table.

"Either Legg made a haul," Cellini said, "or he didn't. In either case, Lansing is not dishing out with information so I'd like to check just how phoney that investment company of his is."

"Check how?" asked the bookie.

Cellini took from his pocket the key-ring he had lifted. "One of these fits the Lansing office and you claim you were pretty handy with safes."

"I begin to catch," said Mack slowly. "All right. I'll play along."

"Fine. Let's go out and get something to eat. We've got a couple of hours to kill."

The Greek came back and Mack asked to borrow his museum-piece Webley.

"No, no. I need it to geeve that man shootings."

"Come on. He's after us—not you."

The Greek acknowledged the point and gave in. Cellini and Mack had another brace of drinks and left.

MACK BANGED LONG and hard on the rear service door of the Tower Building. After several minutes, the night watchman opened it, a cautious hand over the revolver on his hip.

"Oh, it's you," said the watchman after he had identified the bookie's big figure. "Can't let you in. We've been having us a robbery. Besides, I'm broke."

"You're passing up a sure-fire thing, Harry," said Mack persuasively. "It's for the seventh, tomorrow."

Mack pulled the Pacific edition of the Chicago racing form out of his pocket and beckoned the watchman to a transom light two doors down. Despite himself, the watchman followed the bookie and read the form over his shoulder. It never seemed to occur to him why they could not read the form by the overhead light of his own door. He was absorbed.

With his shoes in one hand, Cellini Smith silently left the

shadows of the building and slipped through the door just a few feet behind the watchman's back.

He could spot no immediate hiding place so he padded up the rear stairway and lay down flat on the first landing. After a few minutes he heard the watchman come in, lock the door, and move down the hallway. He waited another minute, then let in Mack.

Noiselessly, they mounted the eight flights to the darkened offices of the Lansing Investment, found the right key on the chain, and entered. Cellini locked the door from the inside. They waited some time before they felt assured nothing stirred in the hallway or adjoining offices, then snapped on a desk lamp.

Cellini led the way inside the railing. "There," he said in lowered tone. "That's the strong-box Lansing claims Legg cracked."

Mack dropped on his knees before it. The safe was large and imposing and of recent vintage.

"Four tumblers," the bookie muttered. "No ordinary chrome steel either. Work on it all day with an acetylene torch and get no place. I guess you're right, Cellini."

"About what?"

"Them hinges are the originals. Jimmy Legg didn't blow this baby. I'd think twice before trying it myself. She's probably wired from the back and if you'd try moving her to get at the wires the alarm would sound off."

Cellini nodded with satisfaction. "That's the way I figured. Now let's try to find the box that Legg *did* crack. We'll start with Lansing's office first."

They switched off the desk lamp and went into Lansing's

office, closing the door before snapping on the lights.

They did not have long to search. Behind a Currier and Ives print they found a small wall safe. Its door was glossy and untarnished, as if new.

"This is the baby all right," said Mack. "Just about Jimmy Legg's speed, too."

"Think you can manage it?"

"Sure. And I don't need soup. All I want is a needle."

"A needle?" repeated Cellini, puzzled.

"Yeah. An ordinary sewing needle. Maybe we can find it in a secretary's desk."

Mack went out and returned a minute later. "Here it is. It's a little thick but maybe it'll work."

He clenched the needle by its eye between his front teeth and placed the point over the lock, his forehead touching the safe. Then he began to turn the combination slowly, feeling every tremor through the highly sensitive nerves of his teeth.

Cellini watched with interested admiration as the bookie grunted through clenched teeth each time he felt a tumbler slide into place. Here was no need for wires or pliers or even nitro. Mack's kit was a sewing needle.

Finally, the bookie stood up and let the needle fall from his mouth. "That does it."

Cellini went to open the safe door when Mack's voice halted him. "Not so damned fast."

Pointed at him was the Webley the bookie had borrowed from the Greek. "What's eating you?" asked Cellini quietly.

"The eight hundred smackers Jimmy Legg still owes me," stated Mack harshly. "I didn't come here and open this box to do you no favor."

"I didn't think so."

"That's right, Cellini. So I'm counting out my eight hundred first." Without taking his eye off Cellini, he reached behind him with his free hand, flipped the safe door open and stuck his huge paw into the opening.

It was empty.

Cellini felt like having a good belly laugh but was afraid that the watchman might be making his rounds nearby. Instead, he said: "Put up the rod, Mack. Fate is forcing you to stay straight. Whatever was in there, it looks like Legg beat us to it."

5

Cooked Goose

AFTER FIVE MINUTES of searing concentration, Cellini Smith felt virtually certain that that thing next to the bed he was lying on was a telephone. Carefully, he lifted the receiver, brought it to an ear, and asked something. A honeyed voice informed him that he was in a downtown hotel and that it was ten in the morning.

He managed to replace the receiver and suddenly remembered what he was doing there and why someone seemed to be carrying out a scorched earth policy inside his head. It had reason.

After drawing a blank at the Lansing Investment offices, he and Mack had decided to go find Manny Simms—before Simms found them. They had gone from gin-mill to gin-mill but could not find the hood. And at each place they had drinks and after a while forgot to search for Mr. Simms.

Vaguely, he remembered phoning Winnie Crawford at three in the morning to find out if she got her money by blackmailing Lansing Investment. The reply was colorful—so much so that he felt the blackmail hunch wasn't far wrong.

Somewhat less vaguely, he remembered deciding to sleep at a hotel, safely distant from any visit by Manny Simms during the night. And he did not at all remember what had happened to Mack. The bookie had spent most of the evening bemoaning the $800 he had lost through Legg's murder and yearning to get his hands on Manny Simms and Winnie Crawford—though for different reasons.

However, the night of alcoholic search had not been entirely fruitless. Nagging at Cellini's mind had been the problem of why Jimmy Legg troubled to conceal apparently innocent items such as a spool of wire, pliers, and hammer in the icebox of his apartment. Somewhere between the double Scotches the answer had come. It added up beautifully.

Slowly, Cellini eased himself out of bed and floated into the bathroom. A needle shower helped a little and the black coffee and bromo in a café downstairs finally decided him against suicide. He tried several nearby parking lots before finding his car and then made for his office.

CELLINI SMITH SAT behind his desk nursing both the hangover and the wisp of an idea that was beginning to form about Legg's murder. And that was its one fault—that it did everything but solve Legg's murder. It was an idea founded on the assumption that the Lansing Investment Company was a crooked outfit.

The phone sounded. Cellini lifted the receiver and gave a weak "Hello."

He heard that horrible, sawmill voice of Howard Garrett's secretary giggle coquettishly and then tell him to wait a moment as she plugged the lawyer into the board.

A click and Jimmy Legg's mouthpiece was saying: "Mr. Smith, I am well aware that we dislike each other. Nevertheless, since you're working on the murder of my former client, I feel there's an explanation due you."

"Goody. Let's have it."

"As you know, I represented James Legg in court on that Lansing Investment affair and yesterday you found me in those very offices waiting to see Mr. Lansing. That may cause you to suspect something."

Cellini's headache wasn't getting any better. "Come on, Garrett. There's a shortage of gas, so save it."

"The point is, Mr. Smith, that I was up there because I'm a stockholder in the Lansing Investment Company."

"How come Lansing didn't object to your defending Legg?"

"As a matter of fact, Mr. Lansing was glad to have me handle the case because he didn't want Legg punished. He thought I might be able to handle it discreetly."

"What did you do when Legg was arrested? Chase after him to let you be his mouthpiece?"

"Certainly not. That's unethical. He got in touch with me."

Cellini almost felt like laughing. "Lansing would be glad to have you defend Legg just at the moment Legg decides to pick you."

"It's not that absurd," Howard Garrett conciliated. "Mr. Lansing got in touch with Jimmy Legg and asked him if he wished to have me for counsel."

A sweet mess, thought Cellini. A man is robbed and then goes to the burglar to recommend a mouthpiece to spring him. He asked: "Are you going to defend Manny Simms when he comes up for trial?"

"Certainly not."

"Did you or Lansing shell out the dough for Manny's bail?"

"Mr. Smith, I called to give you information as a favor. I regret that you're not sufficiently civilized to be polite about it."

"You didn't phone because you wanted to do me a favor."

"Perhaps you know better, Mr. Smith. Why did I phone you?"

"I don't know. But one thing I do know is that you and Lansing and that whole investment outfit will never have to worry about sunburn—you're too shady for that."

Cellini let the receiver drop into its cradle thinking that his parting shot would have been much better if he didn't have to cope with the damned hangover. He heard heavy, stumbling steps in the hallway outside and a moment later the door pushed in and Mack entered.

The giant bookie gaped silently at Cellini. He made a ludicrous picture. One side of his face was shaved and the other bearded, with lather still smeared over it. His jaw trembled as if from some nervous tic.

"I just heard about Winnie." Mack spoke as if the words were being jerked out of him. "She's dying. She's been shot."

CELLINI POUNDED MACK with questions until he had, at last, a coherent picture of what had happened. As little as twenty minutes before, there had been several shots in Winnie Crawford's apartment at the Hamilton. A woman in an adjoining apartment had rushed out to see the back of a man disappearing around a bend in the hallway. She looked into Winnie's apartment to find the blonde on the floor, still alive but with three bullets lodged in her.

An ambulance from a nearby hospital made the round trip in record time and within ten minutes Winnie was on the operating table. An interne, who placed his bets through Mack, recognized Winnie and phoned him at the barber shop. The bookie had immediately come up to Cellini's office.

Winnie had evidently tried to put up a fight for the .45 was found by her side. No hope was held for her and her assailant had escaped.

Cellini felt a little sick. He remembered the clumsy way she held the big gun in her hands and thought that, unlike Legg, she was too decorative to be killed. But at last there was something to work on. It was now 11:25 and the murder had occurred at 11:05. It would be easy to check the alibis of the four persons who might have gunned for Jimmy Legg and Winnie Crawford.

Mack's voice broke hoarsely into Cellini's thoughts: "What the hell are you waiting for? I told you she's dying!"

They hurried downstairs and crowded into the coupé. "Which hospital?" asked Cellini.

"Who said anything about going to the hospital? We can't help her. Drive to the Greek's. I know I need a drink."

Cellini considered that to be sensible and turned over the starter. They reached the Greek's a short while later and entered. It was early and they had the place to themselves. The Greek set out drinks and asked for the ancient Webley Mack had borrowed. After he got it he preserved a discreet silence for he saw that something was up.

Mack went to the wall phone and dialed his interne friend at the hospital. He returned to the bar, shaking his head. "Winnie ain't got a chance to pull ahead. Too big a handicap. Carrying too much weight."

"Sure you don't want to go down to the hospital?"

"No. The doc promised to phone me here."

"Good enough." Cellini tried his drink and found that it helped his hangover jitters. 11:05, he thought. He had to find out where the four men were then—the four men who had a motive to murder Winnie Crawford. Lansing, Howard

Garrett, Manny Simms, and the bookie himself.

The phone rang and Mack jumped for it. When he came back, unashamed tears cut two trails down his tough cheeks. "She's dying, Cellini. My darling's rounding the three-quarter mark." The bookie started to extol Winnie Crawford's physical virtues when the sound of the phone interrupted him fifteen minutes later. He returned with another bulletin. "No hope. She's nearing the home stretch."

It was another half-hour before the phone rang again. This time, Mack's voice was barely distinguishable. "Winnie just crossed the wire." He reached for the bottle and drank out of it.

They drank without speaking and it was the Greek who finally broke the silence. "Do you remember thees Seems, thees people who do the shootings yesterday?"

"What about him?" asked Cellini impatiently.

"He comes now—with beeg gun."

CELLINI AND MACK whirled too late. Manny Simms was entering the door, toothpick in mouth and the chatter gun in his hands. The torpedo who had been with him yesterday, flanked him now, sporting an automatic.

"All right," barked Manny Simms. "Line up against that wall and tell me where you got it."

Cellini and Mack backed slowly toward the wall. They were dealing with a known killer. Manny Simms spoke to the torpedo.

"You take care of the bartender," he growled.

"I show you who takes good cares!" The Greek was fighting mad. The Webley was in his hand, leveled at the advancing torpedo, and he pressed the trigger.

Nothing happened.

The rusted, obsolete weapon was jammed. The Greek delivered a Hellenic curse. He hurled the Webley at the torpedo and, that done, dived behind the bar just as the automatic planted a bullet in the mirror behind him.

"What the hell's the matter with you?" snapped Manny Simms, his eyes not leaving Cellini and Mack. "Stop piddling around."

"Leave him to me, Manny."

The torpedo leaped lithely onto the bar, after the Greek. From behind the bar an arm arced up in a swift, sure curve and the torpedo tumbled back, an agonized scream escaping him. Buried three inches deep into his shoulder was an ice pick.

Manny Simms tried a quick look in back of him to see what had happened. It was the break Cellini had waited and hoped for. At that same instant he dived forward, football fashion, and caught Manny Simms in the midriff, bearing him to the ground. Simms tried to angle the clumsy Thompson sub at Cellini. But the weapon dropped as his arm was twisted back and up.

Mack was there now and he yanked Manny Simms away from Cellini. A queer, chilling laugh escaped him. Now he could do something about Winnie Crawford's murder.

On the floor, the torpedo stirred and moaned. Mack's foot lashed out and caught him under his chin, returning him to unconsciousness with a crack that indicated a broken jawbone.

"Hold it, Mack," said Cellini. "I want to ask Simms a couple of things first."

"Sure. He'll tell you anything you want to know."

Cellini said to Simms: "What did you mean before, when

you asked us where we've got it?"

Manny's yellow face stared impassively, registering no emotion. His shoulders tried to move in a shrug but they were vised tightly by Mack's big paws.

"Come on," said Cellini. "Did you want to know where we've got the stuff that Jimmy Legg stole from Lansing Investment?"

The same dead-pan stare.

Cellini asked: "Where were you at eleven five this morning when Winnie Crawford was shot?"

This time Manny's lips moved to say: "I been third-degreed by experts."

"Plenty time we got to become experts," stated the Greek who stood by them now.

He and the bookie dragged Manny Simms around one end of the bar. Mack said: "You killed the only twist I ever loved."

Simms made the mistake of laughing. Mack's arm moved and the hood dropped down. "Did you kill Winnie Crawford?"

There was no answer from the floor. Cellini saw the bookie's face twitch and was glad that his name wasn't Simms. Mack's eyes scanned the back-bar searchingly and saw a tray. "What's that?"

"Dry ice," replied the Greek.

"Good. That'll be just fine to start with." Mack sat on Manny Simms' chest and the Greek held down the legs. Mack ripped open the hood's jacket and shirt and clamped one hand over his mouth. With the other hand he inverted the tray of dry ice on the bare stomach.

Cellini strayed away. He tried not to hear the sudden writhing and stifled moans, tried not to imagine the ice searing and burning into Manny Simms' belly.

He felt he had to keep himself busy and phoned the barber shop where Mack claimed to be when Winnie was shot. There was no doubt of it, a barber replied to the question. Mack was there at 11:05, taking bets and waiting for his turn in the chair.

When Cellini turned away from the phone again it was over. Manny Simms, a tough hood a short while before, was now a gibbering, babbling mess—confessing to the murder of Winnie Crawford, moaning about crooked deals pulled by Lansing and Howard Garrett with the investment outfit.

Relenting, the Greek poured some olive oil over the burned, tortured flesh. The bookie, a little tired now that it was all over, held on to Simms and dully asked why and how he had killed Winnie.

Cellini said: "That's enough, Mack. You're doing fine. Let's go see Haenigson."

Cellini tried the phone again and was informed that the detective-sergeant was up at the investment company offices, seeing Mr. Lansing.

IT WAS A strange-looking crew that was ushered into Lansing's private office by the secretary. Leading them was the torpedo, his shoulder bandaged by one of the Greek's soiled napkins, his hands cupping the swollen, broken jaw. Behind, stumbled Manny Simms, every slight motion agonizing torture as clothing brushed against his skin. And bringing up the rear, Cellini and Mack, disheveled, sleepless, but satisfied.

"What's this?" asked Ira Haenigson. He was there with a couple of his men, dishing out what looked like a warm grilling to Mr. Lansing and Howard Garrett, the attorney.

"Here's your murderer," replied Mack.

"Manny Simms?" Haenigson's brows arched. "I was under the impression that Simms was under Judge Reynolds' bench while Jimmy Legg was being killed."

Mack, a little crestfallen, started to explain that it was probably the torpedo who did the Legg job but Cellini waved him into silence and turned to the Homicide man.

"It wasn't Simms who did the murders. I just brought him up here to show that we made him see the light and he's been talking. You can take them away to be fixed up."

"I don't like that kind of rough stuff, Smith, but we'll discuss it later." Haenigson nodded to one of his men and Simms and the torpedo were led out. "Now, who did you say the murderer was?"

"Not counting Simms, it has to be either Mack, or Lansing or Howard Garrett."

"Unless it was someone else. Thanks for the tip, Smith."

"They all had motive," Cellini continued, ignoring him. "Mack here, might have wanted to cut a slice of the blackmail for himself that I'll tell you about later. However, his alibi looks good. I'm pretty sure he was at a barber shop shortly after eleven this morning while Winnie Crawford was being killed."

"Thanks, pal." The bookie said it not sarcastically but threateningly. Lansing and the attorney were cautiously silent.

"Mr. Garrett's alibi," said Haenigson, "is equally good for the Crawford killing. It so happens he was in his office phoning me at just about that time."

"I know," nodded Cellini. "I happened to talk to him, too, around that time. That leaves Lansing."

The Homicide man's voice fairly purred. "He was at a board meeting, at the bank."

Cellini frowned. It was the kind of alibi that could be easily checked and Lansing wouldn't have tried it had it not been true. But still, one of the three alibis *had* to be a phoney.

Haenigson smiled benignly. "Let there be more revelations, Smith."

"Sure. Some I know, some is guesswork—but it's the only possible explanation. In the first place, Howard Garrett is the chief stockholder in this investment outfit and he and Lansing have been milking the company, juggling the books, for some time now."

Haenigson made a face. "You're a back number, Smith. And I didn't have to use torture methods to find it out."

"And you didn't have to stand in front of a sub-machine gun. But here's something else. Some time ago there had to be a murder connected with this place—a murder committed by Manny Simms."

THIS TIME THE Homicide man's voice was serious. "Lansing and Forrester," he murmured. "That's what this place used to be called a couple of years ago. Forrester just disappeared and I remember we had Simms on the carpet for it but we couldn't prove anything."

"Perfect," said Cellini. "Lansing had his partner killed by Simms when his partner found out that he and Garrett were juggling the books."

"Preposterous!" snorted Mr. Lansing.

"Shut up!" countered Garrett.

"But," Cellini went on, "Lansing also knew that once Simms did such a job for him he'd be blackmailed the rest of his life so, at the same time, he got proof that Simms had murdered his partner. Whether it's in the form of an actual snapshot of the killing, a written confession, or something else, we'll know later because that's one of the things Jimmy Legg stole from here. Understand?"

"I'm still listening, Smith."

"Then Winnie Crawford got a job here through Mack and soon she was playing office wife to Lansing. Being in a privileged position, she discovered that Lansing and Garrett were taking their gullible investors to the cleaners. So she simply left Lansing's couch, decided that all men were beasts, and blackmailed Lansing into supporting her in style."

"My relationship with Miss Crawford was purely personal," Lansing protested.

"I'll bet," remarked the detective-sergeant dryly.

"Enter now Jimmy Legg," continued Cellini. "He had been the first rung on Winnie's ladder to death. When he saw Winnie in clover without a panting male around, he was able to figure out the blackmail angle and decided to cut in."

Again Lansing protested. "This whole thing is based on the assumption that Mr. Garrett and I have misappropriated company funds."

"Grow up," said Howard Garrett wearily. "By tomorrow a dozen accountants will be going over the books with a fine comb and you know what they'll find. But unless you keep talking we'll only take a larceny rap and not murder."

Ira Haenigson rubbed his hands together. "And that," he announced, "is what I call making progress."

Cellini picked it up again. "So Legg burgled this place. He knew that blackmail material wouldn't be in the regular box so he looked around and found a small safe behind that picture."

"How did *you* know there's a wall safe behind there?"

"Sheer deduction," said Cellini blandly. "Anyway, Legg cracked it and found the real books—the ones showing what Lansing and Garrett have stolen. So when Legg was picked up by the police he told Garrett that if he and Lansing wanted to stay out of jail they'd better mother him. That's why Garrett became mouthpiece for a small-timer like Jimmy Legg."

"You're on the right track, Smith—for a change."

"Then Manny Simms became panicky because he knew Legg had also gotten the proof of his having murdered Lansing's partner. So he pulled that trick of forcing the judge to release Legg because taking such a rap is better than going up for murder. Simms had to get Legg away from the police where he could be killed at leisure and the stolen stuff recovered."

The Homicide man interrupted: "Where is that stolen stuff?"

"I'll tell you later. It's obvious why Legg was killed. In the meantime, Winnie had hired me, trying to find out what it was all about and when Manny Simms saw me hanging around Legg's house he thought I had recovered the loot and tried to chop me down."

"And why," asked Haenigson, "was Miss Crawford killed?"

"The murderer knew that Legg intended hiding out at Winnie's house and got the idea he might also have hidden the loot up there. So one of these three men here went up to Winnie's house to search and when she showed fight—simply killed her."

"Very beautiful," said Ira Haenigson, "but for one thing."

"What's that?"

"You still haven't named the killer."

CELLINI SMITH NODDED and glumly studied the tips of his shoes. One of the three alibis for 11:05 that morning had to be wrong. Lansing was at a board meeting—with many witnesses. Mack was at the barber shop—also with witnesses. The lawyer was in his office—and there could be no question of that because the sawmill voice of his secretary could not be mistaken.

Cellini looked up to find Ira Haenigson standing over him. "It's my turn, Smith. I've warned you before that I'll break you and this is my chance. I found your prints all over Jimmy Legg's apartment and I'm pulling you in."

The detective-sergeant meant it. There was no doubt of that in Cellini's mind.

Cellini stood up. "I want to make a call first."

"Don't try any Indian rope tricks, Smith."

"Since you're arresting me, I want to let my lawyer know." He went out to the front office, a cop trailing, and dialed his number at one of the desk phones. The girl who answered informed him that the lawyer was at home.

"Give me his home number," said Cellini. "I'll ring him."

The girl replied: "Would you want me to call him and connect you two? It would be no trouble."

Cellini gripped the phone hard. "How can you do that?"

The girl laughed. "Oh, that's just an across-the-board call. You can connect two outside calls on most any P-B-X board. It's—"

"I love you," said Cellini, "and I want you to marry me." He returned to Lansing's office, a happy grin dominating his face. He walked up to Howard Garrett and said bluntly: "You're going up for murder and not larceny after all."

"Indeed?"

"Indeed. When you came out of the courtroom with Jimmy Legg you followed him to the drugstore and listened while he called me and Winnie Crawford. You heard him say he was going to the Hamilton Apartments through the side alley. Legg probably made sure nobody was following him to the Hamilton but you were already waiting there for him."

The lawyer didn't turn a hair. "And I suppose you'll deny talking to me and my secretary this morning just about when Miss Crawford was murdered."

"On the contrary. Right after you killed Winnie you made for the first phone and you had your secretary ring Haenigson and myself immediately on an across-the-board call to establish your alibi. Hearing your secretary's voice we naturally assumed that you were in your office. You thought—"

"All right." Howard Garrett's voice was very tired. "I know when I'm finished. Please don't lecture me."

Cellini beckoned Mack. "That's that. How about a drink at the Greek's?"

Ira Haenigson waved him back. "I don't know how you weasel your way out of these things, Smith, but I still want to know where that stuff is that Jimmy Legg stole from here."

"Certainly," said Cellini graciously. "Remember the pliers, hammer, and spool of wire hidden in Legg's icebox?"

"What about it? We looked through the whole place."

"But you didn't figure why Legg thought it necessary to hide those items. The stuff is hanging from wire underneath the outside sill of a window in Legg's apartment—probably the window facing the empty lot."

A Taste for Murder

*Cellini knew something was cooking at Hooper's
drive-in eatery the minute he laid eyes on
the three glamor-girl carhops—including a
bit of Russian dressing named Tanya. But
when the beefy chef started carving assorted
cold-cuts out of the customers, the kill-wise
shamus hastily decided to move on—before
too many crooks spoiled Cellini's broth.*

1

Drive in and Die

HE WORKED THE wheezing coupé across the paved lot toward the drive-in, circled around to the north side, and stopped. He chose the spot from experience for the other end was to the windward side of the kitchen odors and in a line with the blinding illumination from the neon sign. In addition, from his vantage point on the north side, he could sight along the front of the drive-in.

And that was what he wanted.

The neon sign above read, *Hooper's Number 7*, and the building was a circular affair with lots of chromium and glass. On the front curbing of the drive-in were three worldly-eyed girls who jumped with trays at the blast of a horn only until such time as they got their big break in pictures.

One of the carhops took in the make and the year of the newcomer's car and tabbed it for a nickel tip. The blob of red on her face drew wide in a tired smile and she came forward. She wore too-tight slacks, too-loose blouse and a military cap topped by hair that was blond by the grace of peroxide.

She slipped a card behind the windshield wiper, listing Hooper's seventeen delicious desserts, put a foot on the running board and then the smile took it on the lam.

"Oh, it's you again."

The lettering on her loose-fitting blouse read *Berenice*.

He leaned out of the car window and looked at her appraisingly. She wouldn't be bad, he decided, if she took a little trouble with herself. Get rid of that fine down on the chin, don't try for the cupid-bow effect with lips as straight as these, and arch the brows. It would give her a cute, impish effect instead of the soft, feminine one for which she strove. She was too hard to fool anyone in her present get-up.

"I'm tired of it," said Berenice.

"Of what?" he asked.

"What do you want from me?"

"I'm a talent scout, Berenice. We're looking for new faces. We need a beautiful girl who has a photogenic face and four good tires."

"Did you ever get past the first grade, mister?"

"In a way."

"Then maybe you can understand this." She spelled out four letters.

He wagged his head disapprovingly.

"Why do you keep coming back here?" The loose blouse heaved angrily. "I don't like it."

"I told you I was—"

"You told me you were a private detective."

"I am," he said.

"Well, private dicks don't go around announcing what they are. You're either a liar or you're trying to hang something on me. Get this, mister: I'm just a carhop and I don't go in for any sidelines. Maybe it's Tanya you want but not me."

"Simmer down, Berenice. I should think you'd be glad to see me. Every time I come in, I tip you fifteen cents on a twenty-five cent bill. Not everybody who comes in here throws around money as if it was money."

The guy in the sedan had a steak-knife buried in his back.

"Sure you tip me but you never touch your sandwich and coffee. I don't even believe you're a private detective." She threw it at him expectantly, hoping to get information.

"Bring me a sandwich and coffee," he said in reply. "And if I were you, I'd put the lipstick on a little straighter. You look as if you have a nosebleed."

The blouse angled up sharply but, as she was ready to lash out, a car slid into the space next to the coupé. Berenice's words, as she spoke, were whispered but no less pungent.

"Don't ever bother me again, mister. Get that? I can't stop you from coming here but Tanya or Myrtle will serve you. Not me. Just—"

"Any trouble?" It was a man's voice from behind Berenice.

He wore a white hat that looked like a miniature mosque, and a gray-white apron. He was the chef at Hooper's No. 7 Drive-in. In his hand was a meat cleaver.

"Nothing, dear," said Berenice hastily. "I'll let Tanya take care of him." She walked away.

The chef stuck his head inside the coupé and brandished the cleaver. "I saw you getting funny with my wife, buddy. Don't try it any more."

The other took in the dirty neck and blackened fingernails and his throat gagged at the thought of all the food he had eaten here. "I won't try it any more," he promised.

TANYA WENT TO the coupé. Unlike Berenice, she used makeup to the best possible advantage. It was already dusk and one of the Hooper Drive-in rules permitted carhops to put on their slacks after 5 P.M. But Tanya still wore shorts. She knew she had good legs.

"Your order, please." The Russian carhop's voice was husky and only faintly accented.

The man in the coupé took in the tall girl coolly. She looked like one of the low numbers of the upper four hundred and he wondered what kept her hustling trays at sixteen a week with tips. She was invented for better things—and she knew that too.

He also wondered what had made Berenice say that a private op would want her.

"Have you been working here long?" he finally asked.

"Over a year."

"Do you know anyone called Al Moore?"

"Alfred Moore?" Tanya considered it and shook her head. "I

understand now why Berenice wouldn't serve you. You annoyed her with questions."

"Berenice is just excitable."

The carhop laughed. "She is and she has no sense of humor. Once she slapped a customer because every time he came in he asked for a crazy eclair."

"What's a crazy eclair?"

"One that thinks it's a Napoleon."

"He deserved to be slapped. But Berenice also has a vigilant husband. He came around and waved a hatchet in my face."

"Hot damn! Those hosbands!" She smiled knowingly and leaned closer. The breeze fluttered her hair against his face.

He said: "I'll have a barbecued beef sandwich and coffee."

She drew away. "On rye?"

"It makes no difference. I wouldn't eat it after seeing that chef's antiseptic habits."

Tanya giggled and left. As he watched the long legs move away, he suddenly realized that she had spoken of the Al Moore she didn't know as Alfred. That was correct. But why not Albert or Alexander?

He slumped back in his seat and a frown crossed the sharp-boned face as he watched Berenice, Tanya and Myrtle service the cars. He could see Berenice look toward the food alcove from the kitchen to the counter. Her husband was not watching and she walked quickly to the coupé.

He said: "Go away. I don't feel like being butchered by that chill-goon of yours."

"Mister, I'm in trouble."

"That lets me out, Berenice. Hot-damn Tanya feeds me now and I'm satisfied." However, his eyes examined her sharply, noting the nervous tautness of her face.

"Charley—my husband—is just jealous and he didn't know. Mister, were you on the level about being a dick?"

"Sure. Why?"

"Well, I need one bad. Can you prove it?"

He pulled a business card from the handkerchief pocket of his jacket and handed it to her. She read the card. *"Cellini Smith, Private Operative."*

"That's right," said Cellini. "What's your trouble?"

"I—you've—"

Before Berenice's stuttering words could frame a sentence, Tanya appeared with a tray. She glared at the other carhop. "First you give him to me and now you're back again!"

"Sure, Tanya," appeased Berenice nervously. "He's yours. I just want to talk to him a little."

"Please, Berenice. You can have him." The Russian hooked the tray inside the car door and strode away scornfully.

"I guess nobody wants me," sighed Cellini. "Except that hatchet man with the nubian fingernails. I still haven't heard your trouble, Berenice."

"That car I was hopping over there. In the back. It—"

Cellini looked and saw a sedan parked toward the far side of the drive-in. "The Chevvy?" he asked.

"Yes," she replied. "I just went there. The man inside. He's dead. He's got a steak knife in his back."

ONLY THE PINPOINT irises of Cellini Smith's narrowed eyes showed as he looked around.

At the moment, there were only some half-dozen cars parked by the drive-in's circular curbing. Another car stood by the wash-rooms, far to the rear of the lot, and an elderly woman sat at the counter munching away. If they had any connection with a steak knife buried in a human back there was nothing to indicate it.

Myrtle was picking up her tray at one of the cars and Tanya's foot beat a tattoo as she nursed her peeve. There was no sign of the chef through the food alcove.

"All right," he finally said. "Someone's got a knife in his back. What am I supposed to do about it?"

Berenice's fingers pecked at his coat sleeve. "I don't want to be mixed up in any murder. If you're really a dick you ought to be able to help me."

"Are you sure he's dead?"

"Of course. The knife got to his heart but I don't want to be suspected.

"I doubt if you'll be suspected unless you've known him before. Have you?"

"This is the first time he came here," replied the carhop.

"That's not what I asked."

"I never saw or spoke to him before."

"That's better even if it isn't truer. I was watching you before when you came away from that car and I saw you stuff something inside your blouse. What was it?"

The carhop shook her head. "I don't know what you're talking about."

"Don't you ever give a straight answer, Berenice?"

"You're crazy! I tell you you didn't see me do anything."

"All right." Cellini looked toward the Chevvy sedan. In the gathering dusk, he could barely make out the figure slumped over the wheel. He noticed that the car was parked not far from the rear entrance to the kitchen—not far from the chef with the homicidal instincts.

"Why do you think the guy parked there?" he finally asked.

"I don't know. Couples usually go there to neck while they feed. Maybe he wanted to be in the dark." She shook her head impatiently. "What difference does it make?"

"Plenty. He's parked too far over. Anybody could have followed him in from the street and knifed him. It broadens the range of suspects to include the whole city. Besides, he's conveniently near that back kitchen door."

He saw that she understood the implication of his words but she said: "What about me?"

"Your best bet, Berenice, would be to call the cops."

"Yes, I know, but I took care of that car and I'd be mixed up in it. They'd pin it on me."

"Then I have another suggestion," Cellini said. "Simply keel over in a faint and let me handle the rest. You'll be carried inside and one of the other girls will find the body."

"Wouldn't the cops catch on to a stunt like that?"

"I'm sure they wouldn't," he said, knowing very well they would.

"I'll go it," she decided.

She removed the tray from Cellini's car, turned to go, and suddenly slumped to the ground. Tray and dishes crashed. Somebody yelled, car doors opened, and feet began to hurry toward the carhop.

Cellini stepped from the coupé and knelt over Berenice. Her eyes were shut and the body limp. He decided it was a good job of fainting. He raised her head with one hand and slipped the other inside her blouse. He felt a roll of paper and quickly dropped it in his pocket.

Others were there by now and they carried her inside the drive-in. "Poor girl"... "Overwork"... "Underpaid"... Cellini stopped listening and returned behind the wheel of his car. He took out the roll of paper from his pocket. They were green and they totaled up to two hundred dollars.

Berenice had lied like a press agent. There was little doubt that she had removed the money from the corpse before asking for help. Perhaps she had also lied about never before having seen the dead man.

Cellini sighted a white cap approaching. It was Berenice's husband. He was a heavy man with powerful arms and thick wrists. His face was flushed with anger.

"I'm delighted you left your battle axe inside this time," Cellini said.

"I saw you! I saw you messing around!" The chef was a hundred ninety pounds of trembling hatred.

"How's Berenice?"

"I saw you messing around her shirt and I'm gonna teach you a lesson you'll never forget."

"I'm carrying a gun, Charley," cautioned Cellini. "I'm not good at those split-second draws you see in cliffhangers but it'll be fast enough to stop you."

"You couldn't scare me in a dive bomber. I'll fix it so you'll never again fool around with a guy's wife!"

Cellini could see Myrtle walk toward the Chevvy around the side. He had hoped Tanya would be the one to take over and find the body. At any rate, Berenice had escaped the job.

"Ten bucks you don't put a hand on me now," said Cellini. Out of one eye, he watched Myrtle stop by the Chevvy. Her shoulders squared and her chest heaved in preparation for a scream.

"You're on because I'm fixing you right now," snarled the chef. He yanked open the car door.

But the chef was wrong for Myrtle's scream, sounding like an air-raid siren, sent him racing toward the Chevvy.

THE SCREAM ALSO brought a traffic cop from the nearby corner who told everybody not to leave. That was enough to stampede most of the customers to their cars and send them racing away. Two of the customers locked fenders, Myrtle pulled a real faint and Tanya sat down thoughtfully on a running board, tugging at her lower lip.

It was some minutes before Cellini could discover that the dead man in the Chevvy was a newspaper reporter named Jimmy Holland—unless the identification on him lied. The pain-twisted face over the wheel was pasty, middle-aged, undistinguished.

Cellini paced off the distance from the Chevvy to the kitchen door. Eleven feet. All in all, it would require barely more than a half-minute for a hot-headed chef, suspicious of a newspaper-man's attention to his wife, to leave the kitchen, do his knifing and return to the pots and pans.

Tanya, her brows still creased thoughtfully, walked up to Cellini. "Is it possible?"

"What?"

"Please," said the Russian carhop impatiently. "I'm not so stupid. I know why you measure the distance from the car to the kitchen door."

"In that case," he replied, "it's very possible that Charley did the job."

"But why should you disturb sleeping dogs? Why don't you let the police do their own work?"

"They'll do it when they get here whether I let them or not. I'm just interested in the cause of justice, Tanya."

"I heard you were a private detective, Cellini." She spoke his name caressingly.

"That's right, but it has nothing to do with the killing. Even private dicks have to eat someplace."

"You still think I am stupid. Who hired you? Emil?"

It required a few moments for Cellini to place the name. Then he remembered that Emil Hooper was the full name of the drive-in owner. He said: "I guess you're not stupid. What's the idea of pulling your boss into this?"

"Merely to let you know I have influence. You mustn't try to be suspicious of me, Cellini, because Emil will watch out for my interests."

He said: "When I spoke to Berenice before, she suggested that I might want to check on you. Why?"

"That Berenice. She is a fool. If you want to check, you can visit me at the Ryerton." She walked away rapidly before he could put more questions. And she must have known that one of them would have asked how come a carhop could stay at the Ryerton where the singles began at seventy a month.

Cellini pushed through the kitchen door. The chef was staring moodily into the sink, doing nothing.

"You owe me ten bucks," announced Cellini calmly.

Charley didn't reply and Cellini walked over to the food alcove. He sighted along one rim of the alcove to the kitchen door and found that it was angled too far over. Persons entering or leaving by the kitchen door could not be kept under observation by the carhops or by someone who was sitting at the counter.

The discovery made Cellini feel better and he turned to find the chef staring at him instead of the sink.

He said, "Don't forget the ten-spot, Charley," and walked out to await the arrival of Homicide.

2

Food for Thought

DETECTIVE-SERGEANT IRA HAENIGSON took over with that casual and bored air of his that missed nothing. But there was little to learn. Jimmy Holland had never before, as far as the carhops could recollect, eaten at Hooper's Drive-in and none of them admitted knowing him privately.

Holland had driven in and ordered a small fillet with a baked potato. After the food was served, he was alone for some fifteen or twenty minutes. It was during that period that he was murdered with his own steak knife. There was little else to be discovered in any preliminary investigation.

One of the cops recognized Jimmy Holland and said he was a small-time reporter who had worked on several papers and was currently doing crime reporting for the *Morning Telegraph*. A call to the *Telegraph* confirmed it.

Cellini Smith gathered this *minuta* of information from the sidelines and shook his head dubiously. A reporter with two bucks in his pocket was a rarity—but one with two hundred! He tried to catch Ira Haenigson's eye but the Homicide man ignored him and he went to sit down in his car. Berenice followed him a moment later.

"Give it back," said the carhop.

"What?" He noticed that she had straightened the lipstick to conform with the shape of her lips. It was a big improvement.

"The money. I want it right now."

"I thought you claimed that you didn't take anything from the body," Cellini said.

"I didn't. That's mine. I had it on me before I served this Holland or whoever he is."

"If you had it on you all the time, why were you putting it into your blouse just as you came here from Holland's car?"

The carhop's hissing reply came through tightly-closed teeth. "You give me that two hundred bucks, you crook. You didn't give a damn about me when you told me to pull that faint. You just wanted the dough. You took advantage of me."

He grinned.

"Let's have it," snarled Berenice, "or you'll be sorry you ever met me."

"What'll you do? Tell the cops?"

"I'll—"

"Here's a proposition," he interrupted. "I'm willing to return that money but only in front of Haenigson. He's the cop in there. What do you say?"

Before Berenice could frame her reply, a basso began yelling: "Smith!"

"That's Haenigson now," said Cellini. "Excuse me." He stepped from the car and entered the drive-in.

The detective-sergeant sat at one of the tables alongside the counter and indicated a chair. Cellini took it, lit a cigarette and returned Haenigson's tired stare.

The Homicide man finally said: "You know what I want so let's have it."

"Sure I know," replied Cellini, "but you wouldn't believe me anyway, so what's the use?"

"Start talking, Smith." The Homicide man wasn't feeling

very friendly today.

"I don't know a thing about the killing. I just happened to come in here for a bite."

"Just for a bite!" Haenigson's voice was charged with sarcasm. "Your big intestine was growling and you just had to eat. And this drive-in was handy. I understand completely."

"Don't you ever eat?" snapped Cellini.

"Not to an *obligato* of knifings."

"Why don't you check? I never left my car until the murder was discovered."

"I've already checked and you left the car."

"Oh, yes," said Cellini. "I did happen to step out of it for a minute or two when the girl who was serving me keeled over in a faint. What of it?"

"It looks like your fine artistic hand—that's what. The girl who fainted by your car is Berenice Stokes and she was the one who first dished out Holland's food. Something's phoney."

"Suppose it was phoney. What would be the point to it?"

"I don't know." Haenigson rubbed his chin and gazed at the other obliquely. "Then Charley Stokes—that's Berenice's husband—seemed to have some kind of fight with you."

"He thought I was flirting with his wife."

"Were you?"

"That's my little secret," said Cellini coyly.

"Uh-huh. Do you come here often?"

Cellini nodded and asked: "How do you figure it?"

"I thought you weren't interested, Smith."

"Just an academic interest, Haenigson, because I'm a dick. It doesn't do my reputation any good to have someone killed right under my nose."

"Sure. It's simply awful. And how do *you* figure it?"

"The crummy chef—that's Charley Stokes—looks good. It would have been harder for one of the carhops to do it but not impossible. Besides, where Holland was parked, anyone could have walked in from the street and done the job with no trouble."

The Homicide man's chair creaked as he leaned back. "So you know nothing about James Holland's murder and you're merely worried about your reputation."

"That's right."

"If you don't mind, I still think you'll be around tomorrow morning to ask whose fingerprints were found on Holland's car."

Cellini used his innocent look. It was rusty.

"Beat it," barked Haenigson.

AS CELLINI SMITH piloted his car through traffic he counted off the personnel of Hooper's Drive-in. First and foremost was Charley Stokes, the chef. His almost maniacal jealousy concerning his wife was peculiar unless there was some foundation. Mild flirtations with carhops were the rule rather than the exception. It made for larger tips. Charley should not mind them—unless he knew, from experience, that these flirtations grew to be less mild.

Then there were the three carhops. Myrtle, a washed-out innocuous girl who probably knew nothing. Berenice— hot-tempered and quite capable of killing—who denied knowing James Holland but who knew enough to take two hundred dollars right off the corpse.

And Tanya! A girl with class and crust. There was but little doubt that she had angles—outside of physical ones. Carhops without angles don't live at the Ryerton. Berenice may have been thinking of that when she said that a private op could be interested in Tanya. Furthermore, if Tanya really knew Emil Hooper, owner of the Hooper Drive-ins, why was she no more than a carhop? And there was still the point that she knew Al Moore's name to be Alfred.

Cellini reached a side street off Pico and stopped. He was parked in front of the modest, two-story, frame house that belonged to Alfred Moore. He walked up the pathway and tried the knocker.

Al Moore, in undershirt, frowned as he saw Cellini. He was a big man with thick, red lips that gave him a perpetual pout.

"I thought I told you never to come here," said Moore.

Cellini pushed by him, entered the Grand Rapids living-room and sat down.

His host followed. "Why can't you take orders? That's what I'm paying you for."

The fifty-dollar retainer Moore had doled out didn't warrant much taking of orders but Cellini didn't mention it. Instead, he said: "I wanted to see you tonight, and didn't want to wait till you came in the office tomorrow."

"What's the matter?"

"I'm throwing over the job," said Cellini with no intention of doing so.

The pout pushed out still further. "Why?"

"I don't like it and there isn't enough dough in it to make me like it. You're too cagy, Moore. Why do you tell me to stay away from your house?"

"What else don't you like?"

"The whole business! You tell me to hang around Hooper's Drive-in to get a carhop suspicious and to let her know I'm a dick. Why? You don't even warn me that the carhop is the chef's wife and he nearly chops me into a salad. Besides, I don't like to keep eating that chef's food. His fingernails are in mourning."

Alfred Moore gazed down at the rug, his square fingers laced over his stomach, looking like a Yogi. Cellini took in the room and reconfirmed his first impression. Redwood and knotty pine—and the quality of the housekeeping wasn't much better. Dust sheeted the furniture and a love seat had been shoved from its place, into the middle of the room, with the rug crumpled up behind it.

Cellini frowned. On second thought, that love seat shoved from its place didn't look like untidiness. It had been pulled away for a purpose. And the purpose seemed to be to find or put something under the rug.

"I don't blame you for wanting to back out," Al Moore finally said with unexpected mildness. "I'd feel the same way in your place. I really would."

"Ration it," said Cellini. "I don't react to that kind of stuff unless it's from someone like Tanya."

Moore laughed a little too loud. "I guess we both know our way around." He stood up and took a bottle of bourbon and two glasses from a cabinet. As he returned, he shoved the love seat back into its place and flattened out the rug. It was a casual gesture, seemingly motivated by nothing more than neatness.

The host poured bourbon. "By the way, Smith, who is this Tanya you mentioned?"

"One of the carhops down there—which reminds me of

another thing I don't like. You told me you didn't know anyone down there besides Berenice and when I asked Tanya she said she never heard of you."

"That's right."

"She knew your first name."

"Oh." Moore sipped his drink and added: "I guess I spoke out of turn."

"Let's hear it the right way."

Moore drained his glass and it was a full minute before he finally spoke. "I can't figure why you got your back hair up. I haven't asked you to do anything illegal."

"I don't know about that," stated Cellini.

"O.K., Smith. Here's the real thing. I'm married to Tanya and I have to get something on her for a divorce. That's why I asked you to hang around the drive-in. Don't ask me why Tanya and I keep it a secret and why she won't give me a divorce but that's the way it is."

"You're married to Tanya," said Cellini, "so you ask me to hang around Berenice. That's reasonable."

"It is. Berenice is her best friend and I knew that if you told her you're a private dick she'd figure out that I was checking on Tanya."

"It still doesn't make sense," said Cellini. "In such a case, Berenice would immediately tell her suspicions to her friend."

"Not Berenice. She'd sell out her own grandmother. Once she figured out what you were doing there she'd offer to sell you information on Tanya."

Cellini lit a cigarette thoughtfully, then started to laugh.

"What's so hilarious?" Moore wanted to know.

"I think you pulled that story out of your bean bag."

"Are you trying to tell me I'm not married to Tanya?"

"Yes."

"Where the—"

Al Moore stopped short as they heard the front door open. A moment later, a woman entered. She was middle-aged, unhandsome, the tight-lipped, severe kind and the clothes matched.

THE WOMAN HALTED, arms on hips, in the center of the room and sniffed her disapproval of Cellini. "I don't like it one bit, Alfred."

"What, dear?" asked Moore in a timid voice.

"Every time I leave the house I find you regaling one of your suspect friends. It is very underhanded."

"Yes, dear."

"If your friends are not worthy of meeting me they are not worthy of knowing you. Well, introduce me."

"May I present Mrs. Moore," said Al Moore unhappily.

Cellini said: "Delighted to meet you, Tanya."

"Tanya! My good man, if you knew me well enough to use my Christian name—which you don't—it would be Bella."

"He was thinking of his own wife's name," put in Al Moore hurriedly.

"But I'm not married," said Cellini brightly.

"His former wife," corrected Al Moore and added quickly, "Mr. Smith was just leaving, dear."

Bella Moore confined herself to a "Hmpfh" and her husband quickly eased Cellini out. They stopped in the vestibule.

Moore's fingers closed over Cellini's arm and though his voice was low it was none the less menacing. "What are you trying to get away with?"

Cellini looked at the hand over his arm. "Drop it."

It dropped.

"I'm not trying to get away with anything," continued Cellini. "You told me you were married to Tanya so I naturally assumed—"

"You knew damned well she wasn't Tanya!"

"So you admit you lied."

"What of it?" demanded Moore. "You're supposed to be working for me, not against me. We're through, Smith. Get that? Keep the dough I gave you and forget the whole thing."

Cellini nodded pleasantly. "It's a deal. By the way, were you alone over here this afternoon?"

"I was, now beat it." Moore opened the door.

Cellini stepped over the threshold. "It's too bad," he said.

"What is?"

"That you were alone during the murder of James Holland at the drive-in."

"Murder of Holland?" repeated Al Moore stupidly.

"That's right. A reporter."

From the living-room came the querulous voice of Mrs. Moore. "Alfred! I will get the miseries if you do not shut that door this instant!"

Al Moore's lower lip thrust out and his mouth dropped with astonishment and a vague, slowly accumulating fear. He shut the door.

Cellini paused, trying to remember the expression on Moore's face. Which was dominant? Astonishment or fear? Had it indicated sheer puzzlement or a knowledge of the reporter's murder? But whichever the case, one thing was certain: Moore would be around asking to be taken back as a paying client.

Cellini shrugged, lit a cigarette, and started across the lawn for his car as another man went by him, going toward Moore's house. He was elderly—certainly over fifty—and wore a windbreaker. He glanced sharply at Cellini as he passed.

Cellini kept going when he suddenly realized that he could no longer hear the other man's steps. Then he heard them again—but they were not going the other way. He was being followed.

Cellini whirled but made no further move. The stranger's right hand was in the pocket of his windbreaker. The windbreaker was thin and worn and there could be no mistaking the shape outlined in the pocket for something as innocent as a pipe. The hand held a gun.

"Is that your car?"

Cellini nodded.

"Get to it and don't start anything."

Cellini walked to the coupé and slid behind the wheel as the other man sat in, next to him. He had taken out the gun now and held it in a knowing way.

"What name did you bless the world with?" asked Cellini.

"Bingham. Randolph Bingham—as if you didn't know." The old man's voice was bitter and resentful.

"Why should I know?"

"I seen you snooping around the drive-in so don't play dumb. I can take your measure any day in the week. Remember that."

"Around the drive-in," repeated Cellini with satisfaction. Maybe this thing wasn't as senseless as it appeared. He asked: "Were you there when Holland was stabbed?"

"I'm putting the questions," said Bingham. "You been at

Hooper's on and off, the last week, and you must be a dick. I want to hear who you're working for."

"Al Moore," said Cellini after he could think of no advantage to gain by concealing it.

"That's what I figgered. Why'd he send you there?"

"I wish I knew the answer to that one myself."

"You're lying!"

"I wouldn't mind telling you if I knew," shrugged Cellini. "That persuader's enough of an argument."

"There's only one argument I want you to learn from this," said Randolph Bingham. "You never seen me around Hooper's. Get it? I ain't going to be fingered for that killing by no dick. Is that clear?"

"Very clear."

The old man slid from the car and waved Cellini to get going.

3

On the Grid

SOMEBODY, OR SEVERAL bodies, Cellini Smith told himself as he cut across Pico, was laying down a smoke screen. But that also had its advantage. Smoke screens aren't laid down unless there is something to conceal.

The injection of Randolph Bingham into the situation cleared up only one point—that things were even less clear than they had appeared at first glance. Perhaps it would have been better to try and jump the old man and take away his gun. But that would have been forcing the issue. Bingham had already made one mistake—becoming a prime suspect by letting it be known that he had been at Hooper's Drive-in at the wrong time—and if he stayed on the loose he was likely to make more mistakes.

Bingham was visiting Al Moore whose own skirts seemed none too clean and who was quite a liar in his own right. Moore could neither prove that it was impossible for him to be James Holland's murderer nor give a suitable explanation for having hired Cellini to hang around the drive-in—that is, some explanation other than the true one.

Nor were Bingham and Moore the only pieces that didn't fit into the puzzle. There was Berenice Stokes, the firebrand carhop who stole two hundred dollars from the reporter's corpse—a corpse that might have been of her own making. There was Charley Stokes, crazily jealous and inclined to go in for carving.

And Tanya. A competent wench who knew the ways of men and no doubt took advantage of the knowledge. She knew Moore but didn't like to admit it. She knew Hooper, himself, and liked to admit it.

Reminded of the owner of the drive-ins, Cellini stopped by a drugstore, consulted a phonebook, then headed for Beverly.

Some minutes later he was using the knocker on the front door of Emil Hooper's home. A butler opened the door and regarded Cellini none too respectfully.

"Mr. Hooper. Cellini Smith calling."

Cellini stepped into the vestibule and waited until the butler returned with the information that Mr. Hooper didn't know Mr. Smith.

Cellini said: "Ask him if he knows Tanya."

This produced results. For a moment later, Emil Hooper appeared. It was quite evident that he did not eat at his own drive-ins for he was paunchy and round with a cherubic face. He was dressed in a dinner jacket and you expected the front of his shirt to light up and ask you to smoke El Ropo cigars.

"I am revolted," began Emil Hooper. "I hardly expected Tanya to stoop to this sort of blackmail."

"This *sort?*" asked Cellini. "Then you're accustomed to other sorts from her."

"I do not wish to discuss it. You may tell her to be satisfied with our present arrangement or I'll turn the case over to the police. You must excuse me now for I have guests."

"This has nothing to do with Tanya," said Cellini. "I just used her name to get at you."

Hooper relaxed and smiled reminiscently. "I didn't think she was capable of blackmail pressure. Then what is your purpose?"

"It's about the murder of James Holland at one of your places a few hours ago. I'm a private operative."

"That's a filly of a different tint, Mr. Smith. As for the murder, I know nothing of it. I've never met this unfortunate Holland, and I was in my office the entire day as my secretary will attest. All of which I've told the police."

And none of which Cellini doubted. "What about Tanya?" he said. "Can you help me out there?"

Emil Hooper smirked.

"Strictly off the record," urged Cellini. "Between men."

"Ah, Mr. Smith, I'm not being reticent. It's simply difficult to talk about women like Tanya. You just whistle after them."

"When did you first whistle?"

"She was working for me as a carhop when I first saw her. But I didn't whistle then because Mrs. Hooper was with me."

"Do you still see her?"

"Unfortunately no, Mr. Smith. When Tanya says it is the end then it is the end."

Cellini was puzzled. Here was a prime sucker who was taken for a ride and enjoyed it. "What happened when she said it was the end, Mr. Hooper? What did it cost?"

"She said, 'Emil, I have decided I no longer love you and now you will pay.' Of course I expected it and was even prepared to give her several thousands because it had been worth it to me."

"What did she want?"

"She just asked me to mail her ten dollars each week! That was all. I even had my lawyer waiting if she became exorbitant but the sum is so slight I don't mind sending it to her each week. As men of the world we must admit it was extremely fair on her part."

"We must," said Cellini absently. Here, of course, was the answer to how a carhop came to stay at the Ryerton. Blackmail—but only "fair" blackmail. She chose sums sufficiently insignificant to keep her victims paying and prevent them from making trouble. With Hooper, ten dollars a week was meaningless but over a period of years it became an annuity that counted. And with several such annuities—one, no doubt, from Al Moore—it amounted to a nice nest egg.

Cellini thanked Hooper and left.

THE SIGNS ON Hooper's Number 7 Drive-in were darkened and the place closed when Cellini Smith arrived there. Evidently, serving up a murder was enough of a dish for one day.

Through the saddle of the kitchen door he detected a slit of light. He got out of the car and knocked without results. He tried the door, found it open and entered. Sitting on stools by the range were Berenice and her husband Charley in earnest conversation.

"Pardon the interruption," said Cellini, "though I know I'm welcome."

"You wouldn't be welcome in a flop house," said the chef.

"You must try to like me, Charley. What are you two doing around here with the place closed?"

"What are *we* doing? We work here. What the hell do you want from us?"

Charley glanced at his wife significantly and she said hurriedly: "He didn't come back to see me. I want to get that one thing clear. Smith, tell my husband we never had anything to do with each other."

Cellini laughed. "A gentleman never speaks of such things."

*"Get away from the louse, Charley,
and I'll blow him to hell!"*

"Why, you lousy—"

"Tut, my buttercup. Let us have no recriminations about our past." Cellini sighed. "Let us, instead, discuss that two hundred dollars you stole from the body of James Holland."

"You better give back that dough," barked Charley Stokes.

"Then you know about it? That makes you party to the theft."

"That makes me nothing because she didn't steal it. That was her dough."

"If it's as innocent as all that, I'm willing to return the money in front of the police. I made that offer to your wife before but she didn't seem very ready to accept it."

Neither of them replied. "And how about the ten bucks you owe me, Charley?"

Still no reply. Cellini looked around and walked over to a small roll-top desk in one corner. He pawed among the papers but could find little of interest. They were mostly the nightly reports of the carhops and requisitions for food supplies. In one of the cubbyholes he found a list of the addresses and phone numbers of the personnel of this drive-in and put it in his pocket for future use.

As he was about to turn, two arms twined around him, pinning his hands to his sides. Cellini had noted the chef as a powerful man but the viselike arms that circled him now were stronger than he had thought possible.

"Grab his gun," came Charley Stokes' strained voice.

Berenice's hand slipped into Cellini's jacket and took out the automatic.

"Now grab his wallet and get the dough he stole from us. Quick!"

Berenice moved forward again. Cellini tried twisting his arms and found it hopeless. But it was silly to take this kind of manhandling without trying to fight back. As Berenice again came within range, Cellini planted a foot in the pit of her stomach and shoved. She tumbled back, tripping over a garbage pail.

"You damned fool!" Charley Stokes shouted at his wife. "Get at him from the side."

Berenice's face was twisted with rage, and she did not heed her husband's words. She leaped at Cellini, the gun raised in her hand. As she brought down the automatic, Cellini's head bobbed sideways. With satisfaction, he heard the yell of pain as the barrel smashed down on her husband's shoulder.

During the split second that the chef's shoulder took the painful blow from the gun barrel, Cellini wrenched himself free. He whirled and ducked as the chef sent a heavy skillet past his temple.

Berenice rapidly moved away and, with both hands, leveled the automatic at Cellini. This time she wasn't using it as a club.

She meant to shoot. Cellini leaped for the chef. His one chance was to close in—very close—and not give her a chance to get a straight bead on him.

Charley Stokes was no polished boxer but he knew a few of the tricks in the rough-and-ready school. He ducked Cellini's onrush and jabbed his elbow into Cellini's throat. Cellini stumbled back, choking. His fists lashed out savagely as the chef's full weight hurtled at him, bearing him to the ground.

"Get away, Charley! Get away from the louse! I'll blow him to hell! Get away!"

Neither of the men heard Berenice's screaming voice as they rolled and kicked and slashed. Charley's thumbs clawed for the dodging eye sockets and he tried to crush his opponent with his heavier weight.

Carefully countering the jabbing knees, elbows and probing fingers, Cellini let the chef roll over on him. Then he reached around, grabbed a handful of hair and with sudden viciousness jerked the chef's head at the flooring.

The body on him went limp and Cellini rolled away quickly. He had to be quick if Berenice was not to start pumping bullets into him. He was already hunched to launch the tackle at her legs when he realized that her arms, and the gun, hung loosely at her sides. He looked up to find the reason. Al Moore and the elderly Randolph Bingham were standing in the doorway.

CELLINI STOOD UP. He breathed deeply and then walked over to Berenice and removed the gun from her hand. She neither tried to stop him nor go to the aid of her husband who was beginning to stir on the floor.

"We just got here in time." Al Moore was trying to make his

voice sound pleasant. "She would have winged you sure if we hadn't showed up."

Bingham showed the yellow stumps of his teeth. "Mebbe it's too bad we did show up."

Cellini began to repair the damage to his clothing as well as he could. He said: "Maybe you arrived here in time to help me but that's not why you came."

"No." Moore chose his words carefully. "We came about that reporter's murder. James Holland. When you told me about it you implied I was mixed up in the thing and I wanted to see what was cooking."

Charley Stokes stood up slowly and Cellini let him see that he held the gun now. The chef relaxed and kept quiet.

Tears of frustration or self-pity suddenly began to course down Berenice's cheeks and Al Moore said: "It's all right, Berenice. There's nothing to get excited about."

Cellini asked: "How come you're so friendly with her after asking me to—" *To tail her* he would have completed had not Al Moore cut in quickly.

"Smith, I want to talk to you—outside."

They walked out and stopped on the darkened lot.

"Smith, you have no call to tell Berenice I hired you to check on her."

"I owe you nothing, Moore. You fired me."

"That's what I want to talk about. I was a little hasty this afternoon. I didn't know—"

"That Jim Holland had been murdered?"

"Frankly, yes. I don't want to be tabbed for it."

"And now you want me to find the killer?" asked Cellini.

"No, not exactly."

Not exactly! Not at all was more likely, Cellini thought. All Moore wanted was not to have an enemy, not to have someone going around trying to prove he killed James Holland.

"I'm getting bored with this runaround," Cellini said. "I want to know what this is all about. That old duffer you came here with—Randolph Bingham—shoved a gun in my ribs when I left your house this afternoon and told me he didn't kill Holland."

"Don't mind Bingham. He's a little mixed up but he's one of us."

"One of you? Who are the rest of you?"

"Tanya, Berenice, and her husband Charley. Those three and Bingham and me—we're all in this thing and I'm telling you right now, Smith, don't try to cross us up. You keep working for me but don't try to pull any fast ones."

"Quite," said Cellini. "However, it's about time you gave me a vague idea of what this is all about."

"I can't tell you everything but if you string along with us you'll show a profit. We all will because we're on the trail of something big."

"On the trail of big dough?" fished Cellini.

"That's right. Berenice and her husband and Tanya and me know where there's nearly sixty thousand bucks and we're going after it."

"I thought you said that Old Man Bingham was involved in this thing too."

"He is. He's in on the split but he don't shell out for expenses because he tipped us off on where the dough is."

"That was very kind of the old coot. Why didn't he get it for himself?"

"Because he couldn't swing it alone. It needs a lot of dough. It's buried at the bottom of the ocean and that takes—"

"A sucker to fall for it," finished Cellini.

"I'm no sucker. This is on the level. Besides it should make no difference to you."

"A ship sank with sixty grand," said Cellini more to himself than Moore. "There are five of you trying to get it out and suddenly a reporter named Jim Holland is murdered and you're worried. You're afraid to have the killing mixed up with you because then you might never get the dough. You don't want me to find the killer but you want to keep me on the payroll so I will stay quiet. Is that about it?"

"Not quite," said Moore uneasily.

"Then what is my job? Make it good."

"I'll give you something to do, Smith. There's a map marking the place where this ship went down with the dough. Find it, and it's good for a hundred. My hunch is that Berenice and her husband have it. Or maybe Tanya. It's your job to find it."

Cellini thought of a lot of questions to ask but he knew it would be futile. "What about Bingham? I don't want that old duffer pulling a rod on me every time he wants to play Superman."

"Don't worry about Bingham. I take care of him and he follows my orders. Only yesterday I gave him two hundred dollars."

CELLINI SMITH DROVE downtown, toward the Hall of Justice. He wanted to get the police report on the murder of James Holland without running the Ira Haenigson gauntlet on the following day. It was late now—near ten—and it was hardly likely that Haenigson would still be at the Hall of Justice. Perhaps some underling would give out with information.

As he drove, Cellini thought of the two hundred dollars in his pocket. It was probably the same two C's that Al Moore had given Old Man Bingham. Then Bingham must have given it to Holland, the reporter, and Berenice had stolen it off his body. And he, Cellini, had taken it from Berenice. That much was apparent but the why of it was as clear as the inside of a horse.

Nor did Al Moore's information help clarify much. Four persons—Moore, Tanya, Berenice and Charley—had banded together to fish up some sunken treasure on a tip supplied by Randolph Bingham. A reporter named Jim Holland was murdered, probably by one of them, and Moore hired Cellini to find the map whereby the sunken treasure could be located. Not a very logical sequence.

Cellini reached the Hall of Justice and cramped the wheels to the curb. He walked down the broad corridors toward the Homicide Department, pushed open a door and found Ira Haenigson seated at a desk.

It was too late to retreat and Cellini said "Hello," knowing that attempts to explain his presence would be as useless as bombing a graveyard.

The detective-sergeant nodded to a chair. "So you thought you'd pull a fast one and come down here when I wasn't around."

"That's right, Haenigson, but only because you're so unco-operative. Jim Holland happened to be killed right under my nose and I'm naturally interested in knowing about it."

"Knowing what, for instance?"

"How about prints?"

"The knife handle was smudged. Probably a napkin. Next?"

"How about the car?"

"Nothing important. The carhops and others around the drive-in had their prints on the door but that's to be expected."

"What have you found out about Jim Holland?"

"Only," said the Homicide man casually, "that he and Berenice Stokes were interested in penmanship a few months ago."

"Meaning?"

"That they had a habit of signing auto court registers as a *Mr. & Mrs. Smith.*"

Cellini whistled. "That brings us back to Charley Stokes. He's as jealous as an ant of his hill and if he knew about his wife and the reporter we wouldn't need a better motive."

"Not we—I," said Ira Haenigson. "I still don't see where you come in. You said I don't co-operate and I've given you the information I have. It's your turn."

"I've given you what I have."

"Sure. That Berenice fainted by your car and that her husband thought you were flirting with her. It was a big help. But what about that Russian carhop—Tanya. I heard you two had a long talk."

"All I know about Tanya is that she'd look cute on the half shell."

"Smith, I think you stepped into it up to your neck this time."

"Don't tell me, Haenigson. I know. I've been obstructing justice because I happen to eat at a certain drive-in."

"That's right. You're mixed up in this somehow. When you

show up at the Hall of Justice this time of night you're getting paid for it. Just remember—"

"Remember what?" asked Cellini.

"Beat it, Smith."

4

In a Stew

THE DESK MAN at the Ryerton was either accustomed to men calling on Tanya Danilova this late in the evening or he was too well-bred to exhibit surprise. He worked the switchboard, nodded, and Cellini took the elevator to the eighth floor.

Tanya opened the door, smiled, said that she had expected him to call and led him into the living-room. She wore a floor-length dressing gown that, in Cellini's opinion, could have been more revealing.

It occurred to him that she, also, seemed perfectly accustomed to male visitors this late.

"You have a nice place," he said. "It must take most of your tips to keep it up."

"Yes, but sometimes it is difficult. Carhops don't make as much as you think, Cellini." She sat down next to him on a sofa. "Have you found out who keeled that reporter?"

"No, but it could have been Berenice's husband. She and Holland used to play button-button."

"Hot damn! I didn't think Berenice had the imagination."

"It doesn't need imagination. With a little study and some intelligent application, almost anyone can get the hang of it."

Strong white teeth were displayed as she laughed. "Maybe you are wrong, Cellini, and it does need imagination. Yes?"

"No."

"Oh." She examined him with frank curiosity. "Tell me more

about Berenice and why she fainted all of a sudden this afternoon."

"She knew Holland was dead and didn't want to go on record
as finding the body—especially since they had been play-
mates."

"So poor Myrtle had to find the body."

"That's right. Tell me something about Myrtle."

"She lives at the Studio Club, Cellini, where no men are
allowed. That should tell you almost everything. You have also
seen what she looks like and that should tell you the rest."

"Uh-huh. Her face looks as if she slept in it."

"But I don't look like that. No?"

"Double no."

She pulled at the lobe of his ear. "Then why are you so
strange? You sit six inches from me and act as if I were a sack
of potatoes."

"That, Tanya," he said bluntly, "is because I don't feel like
contributing to the upkeep of this apartment. I don't like to
be taken through any blackmail wringer."

"Ah, that explains it." She sounded relieved.

"That's right. Emil Hooper told me he has you on his mailing
list. And how much does Al Moore pay you?"

"Just twelve little dollars a month."

"I thought you didn't know Al Moore."

"That fib, Cellini, was only because I was afraid Mrs. Moore
hired you to spy on me."

"So you get twelve a month from him and ten every week
from Hooper. How many more payrolls are you on?"

"Not as many as I would like."

"You feel safe talking to me, don't you?"

"Fortunately, Cellini, I never feel safe with any man."

"I mean your racket. How come you talk so freely with me about this blackmailing?"

"Because I am not afraid. It is not blackmail, just—"

"Payment for services rendered?"

"That's right, and I always ask so little—never more than they can afford to pay, so they never make trouble. They think they have made the best bargain and that they took advantage of me but a little from each one all adds up at the end of the year. Tanya is smart, no?"

"Brilliant. Did you kill Jim Holland?"

"Hot damn! You come here only to ask me that?"

"No. I came to search the place."

"Go ahead."

He stood up and began the rounds of the living-room. Tanya followed, the full lips in a cynical smile. He opened commodes, looked behind cushions and felt the linings of the window drapes.

When he realized that the carhop didn't intend asking what he was looking for he said: "I'm hunting some kind of chart or map that Al Moore said might be here."

"Of the money? Moore told you I have—" She stopped short. "That was not nice, Cellini. You try to treek me."

"That's right. Suppose you tell me what it's about."

"No."

The *no* was as definite as a parole board's and he said: "Forget it." He walked into the bedroom, looked under mattress and box spring and began pawing through the clothes closet. It was well-stocked with the best labels. He noted a karakul jacket and asked: "Are you really Russian?"

"I am, but a different kind. Not like the others here in Holly-wood."

"What's the difference?"

"I, Cellini, am not the last of the Romanoffs. I am not even the first and the only kind of wolves that ever chased me were Hollywood wolves."

He sat down at the vanity dresser and opened the drawers. He looked up, caught her smile in the mirror and suddenly realized two things. There was nothing in this apartment that the carhop did not want him to see. He realized, also, that Al Moore wasn't the type to dish out money on some phoney proposition without having all information and papers in his own possession. He stood up.

"Aren't you going to search me, Cellini?"

"I have to search my conscience first and if I find what I expect, I'll be back." He left.

IT WAS CLOSE to midnight when Cellini Smith again parked near Al Moore's house. No lights were showing and if he knew anything of Mrs. Bella Moore they were already asleep.

He took off his shoes, secured a screwdriver and a search-light from the glove compartment and stepped out of the car. He moved down the pathway and froze against the grillwork of the porch as a crate loaded with swing-shifters clattered by, heading for the Valley. When they were out of sight, he mounted the steps and tried the front door. Al Moore had not forgotten to lock it.

No windows fronted the frame house from the porch and he circled the lawn, padded down the driveway and tried the rear door. It too was shut and bolted from the inside.

Dark clouds concealed a new moon and he flicked the button of his flashlight long enough to sight a screen-covered window a few inches above his head. He waited and, as a car passed the house, he dug the point of the screwdriver through the 16-mesh wire in one quick thrust. Another minute to be sure that the metallic rip had disturbed no one, and his fingers probed for the catch inside the screen. He found it, lifted the screen from its hinges and tried the French windows. They were unlatched.

Carefully, silently, Cellini gripped the inside ledge of the window and climbed inside. He stood there, trying to get his bearings. As his eyes became accustomed to the grays and blacks he discovered that he was in the dining-room and started for the front of the house, toward the living-room.

He knew that he would have to leave doors open for a quick exit and that a draft would be caused by the open window. He returned and quietly drew the drapes. He was thankful that the house was two-story for it meant that the bedrooms were upstairs. He knew, too, that his feet, soaked with dew from the lawn, left clear outlines wherever he stepped and that his fingerprints couldn't be missed by a correspondence-school detective. But if his guess was right, Al Moore would not call in the police.

When he reached the living-room he stood there for a long while. He thought he could detect heavy breathing from upstairs. That would be Bella and Alfred in peaceful slumber. Then he walked to the love seat and dragged it to one side. He remembered, from his earlier visit, the crumpled rug and the casual way Al Moore had flattened it out. Here was the place to search first. If a map leading to a dubious fortune really existed, Moore would keep it near himself.

He lifted a corner of the rug and folded it back. He dropped on his knees and his hands slid over the flooring. Nothing but the polished oak. A flash of light confirmed it. He swore silently and, finding that unsatisfactory, felt his way to the cabinet where Al Moore kept the bourbon and tilted the bottle to his lips. It was to be expected, Cellini told himself. Moore would keep nothing really important under the rug for sooner or later Mrs. Moore would be sure to find it there.

Then why had the rug been crumpled up? Suddenly it hit him. The baseboards! He returned to the corner and felt molding and board. At one of the joints, the board gave under pressure. He inserted the screwdriver underneath and pried up. It gave—springing out with a loud snap. Cellini froze. That noise would waken a bank president at midday.

He heard someone stirring, from an upstairs bedroom, then the glass-cutter voice of Mrs. Moore: "Alfred! Alfred! Get up. I heard a sound."

"It's nothing dear," finally came her husband's sleepy response. "Go to sleep."

"I distinctly heard something."

Cellini felt behind the baseboard and found that the plaster and laths had been hollowed out.

"That was probably my stomach from your lousy dinner," Moore said. "Go to sleep."

"Alfred! Get up this instant. I am certain there is a footpad in the house."

There were some restrained oaths but Al Moore was getting up. Cellini's hand felt in the hollow behind the baseboard and found an envelope. He put it in his pocket.

Al Moore spoke again—but this time from the landing at the head of the stairs: "There's nothing here, Bella."

"Not there, you oaf. I heard it from the living-room."

"The living-room!"

Moore's voice was suddenly alert and awake. Cellini knew that Moore had remembered that there was something valuable in the living-room—something hidden behind that baseboard.

It was too late to make a run for the dining-room. A night light had been switched on at the head of the stairs and he would have to cross under it. As Cellini heard the creaking stairway under the pressure of Moore's descending weight, he crossed over to the living room's light switch and stood there, waiting.

He crouched low as Moore's shadowy figure, in a pair of light pajamas, appeared at the entrance. The figure moved forward and reached for the light switch. Cellini suddenly lunged and his fist smashed into Al Moore, south of the border. His client crumpled.

Cellini didn't stop to apologize but ran.

ON HIS BED, Cellini Smith spread out the contents of the envelope. There were three items—including the one Al Moore had hired Cellini to find. It was a chart evidently indicating the spot where a ship had gone down. Cellini could make little of the longitudes and latitudes but it seemed to be somewhere southwest of the Isthmus off Catalina.

The second item was a contract for the rental of a boat called the *S.S. Barracuda*—evidently a fishing boat—for a four-month period. The rental fee was $1200 with options at further rental for $500 a month.

The third item was a page torn from a newspaper. It told of the disappearance of the yacht *Periwinkle* off the California coast. She had been making a run from Acapulco, Mexico, to San Pedro with five hands—and $60,000 in currency aboard her. There were also pictures of two members of the crew and one of them was an unmistakable photograph of that fine job of embalming—Randolph Bingham. The page came from the *Standard*—not the one for which the murdered Jim Holland had worked—and the date-line above read: *December 8, 1941.*

So far, not too good, thought Cellini. On the surface at least, Old Man Bingham was on the level. A boat called the *Periwinkle* had gone down with five hands and five figures in money, Bingham survived it and four others banded with him to retrieve the money. Toward this end they had rented a fishing boat.

But Jim Holland was still knifed.

Cellini reached for the phone, put through a call to a water-front café in San Pedro and when he had his connection, said: "Miguel? This is Cellini Smith."

"Cellini! It's good to hear from you but I haven't got much time. I'm making some imported Scotch."

"Did you ever hear of a yacht called the *Periwinkle?*"

"It sounds familiar but she don't ship out of Pedro."

"How about a fishing boat called the *S.S. Barracuda?*"

"That floating septic tank? Hell yes. She's a lemon."

"What should it cost to rent her?"

"You can pick her up for a hundred a month. She ain't worth more than the Italian navy."

"Could you conduct diving operations on her?"

"I suppose so. If you had the equipment. She's a blunt, squat-nosed tub. Why?"

"Forget it." Cellini pushed back the phone. A hundred a month. That was a far cry from the $1200 being paid for four months. But on the chance that there was a grain of truth in it, somewhere, Cellini made a copy of the chart.

When he was finished, he put away the copy, reached for the phone and dialed again. This time it was Berenice's voice that replied immediately. The Stokes family was staying up late.

"Hello, buttercup. I'm calling to give you some juicy information."

"Oh, it's you!" screamed the carhop. "All I want from you is my two hundred bucks."

"Stop being so mercenary, Berenice. Who steals my purse steals cash. I'm calling about your good name. Can your worthy husband hear us?"

"I want my money! Do you get that?"

"Listen to this one, Berenice. It's good. The minions of the law have found out that you and that murdered reporter—Jim Holland—found bliss in sundry auto courts."

Berenice didn't speak. Cellini said: "Don't you think—" He stopped short and gently put back the receiver. Someone was trying the knob to the apartment's door.

He took out his automatic, tiptoed to the door, and threw it wide. Al Moore stood there—an unarmed Al Moore—and Cellini put away his weapon.

CELLINI SHUT THE door behind Moore and waited. All of his visitor's large frame shook with fury and the fists clenched spasmodically.

"Let's have it, Smith. Right now!"

"Everybody wants something from me. What's your beef?"

"Don't try to mess around with me, Smith. I know it was you who broke into my house tonight! You saw the rug wasn't in its place when you came this afternoon and you saw where I kept my whiskey. Only you would have the nerve to drink my whiskey while robbing me."

"All right. I was there, Moore, but in your interests."

"My interests!"

"Sure. You offered me a C to find the chart marking the place where the ship went down and I found it. Why blame me if I figured out you had it?"

"You give me those papers right now."

"For a hundred dollars," said Cellini. "I've done my part and now you do yours."

"I give you your chance, Smith, now I'm going to beat the hell out of you and enjoy it."

"Well, I won't. Just take it easy, Moore. You're excited because I socked you in your pajama knot."

Moore's reply was to hunch his shoulders and lunge. Cellini side-stepped and his left flicked out. Moore whirled and caught a right on the jaw.

"I'm afraid I'm being a poor host," said Cellini. "Cool down and we'll talk it over."

Enraged, Moore leaped, arms grabbing, with no pretense at defense. Cellini carefully gauged his distance to the square jaw and his shoulders pivoted, with his full weight behind the blow. Al Moore dropped like a Russian barometer.

The phone rang.

It was Berenice again. "I want my two hundred bucks!" she screamed.

Cellini sighed. "The broken record," he said.

"It's your last chance to give it to me, you stinking crook! You're trying to frame me for Jim Holland's murder and you're not going to get away with it. You'll be sorry if—"

Cellini slammed down the receiver with irritation. Some people had one-track minds. He reminded himself to find out what it was that Berenice had meant by his being sorry.

Al Moore pulled himself from the floor, somewhat shaken, and sank into a chair. "It's your round," he said bitterly, "but not the last."

"That's right, Moore. Getting Holland's killer is the last."

"I didn't kill him. I didn't even know him."

"Maybe not but you're in it and your actions will give some district attorney a field day."

"All I want is my property—what you took from me."

"I followed your orders to get it and you promised me a hundred when I did. Let's have it." He extended his hand.

Reluctantly, Moore took out his wallet and passed over several bills in exchange for the envelope.

"That's settled," said Cellini. "Hereafter be careful of the assignments you give me. I have a better idea of what this is about since I went through that envelope but I still have a few questions. I want to hear the answers because I'm mixed up with the murder myself."

"I didn't kill Holland. Ask what you want."

"I want to hear about the *Periwinkle*."

"Bingham knows about that."

"Then we're visiting Bingham."

5

Too Many Cooks

CELLINI SMITH SAT on a kitchen chair in the unsavory two-by-four room and listened to Randolph Bingham object to his presence.

"I don't like it," said the old man. "He ain't in it."

"He is in it," said Al Moore. "He's dealt himself in. He's seen the stuff you gave me."

"It's your fault," Bingham barked. "You had to go hire him because you didn't trust me or the rest. Well, it's your dirt so you can sit in it. I ain't going to split the dough with him."

"Let's get something straight," Cellini put in. "I want no part of the sixty grand that went down with the *Periwinkle*."

The old man laughed and turned to Moore. "He's only one and we're two. Let's take him before he wrecks the whole thing. He knows too much and we'll fix it so he forgets it."

Moore didn't seem too anxious and Cellini said: "You're in shirt sleeves, Bingham, and I can see you're not carrying a rod and I know Moore isn't. Well, I am."

"You're lying!"

"Maybe, but you can't be sure. I told you I don't want to be cut in on the dough. I just want to hear your end of the story because the cops are looking for a patsy for the killing and I don't want to be it."

"I think we should tell him," said Moore. "He knows most of it already."

Bingham surrendered. "O.K., if it'll get rid of him."

"I want to hear about that yacht," said Cellini. "The *Peri-winkle*."

"There ain't much. We come up from Acapulco carrying sixty grand and everything went smooth till we got off Catalina."

"What were you doing on the boat?"

"I got on in Mexico. I was working on a tanker and when we hit Acapulco I was offered a job to help bring the *Periwinkle* up at double salary and bonus. So I jumped ship."

"Who offered you the job?"

"The mate. Later he told me the boat belonged to one of those Mexicans who didn't like the way the elections come out and things got too hot for him. So he skipped with all his dough. That's where the sixty grand come in. I saw this Mex after we got out to sea but it was supposed to be a secret that he was aboard her. That's why the newspaper accounts never mentioned him when he went down."

"Go on."

"Like I said," Randolph Bingham continued, "it all went all right till we got off Catalina. The *Periwinkle* was a good boat but she had a lot of wrinkles and the skipper didn't know how to handle her in rough water."

Al Moore stood up to open a window and Cellini said: "Stay where you are. Go on, Bingham."

"It all happened in fifteen minutes. We was going pretty fast with the wind behind us and we got into a heavy following sea and we began to surf-board. The skipper tried to ride it out but the sea kept pushing us faster. Suddenly, her nose went under and she broached sideways into the trough and capsized. *Pfft*. Just like that. Straight down, nose first, with all hands except me. A boat'll do that if she ain't constructed right."

"How did you get out of it?"

"I was standing on the prow when it happened. I found myself in the water, managed to grab hold of a piece of wreckage and floated into a cove on Catalina."

"How come the papers listed you among the missing?"

"When the Coast Guard come across some wreckage from the *Periwinkle* they figured all went down because I didn't report myself. Nobody saw me float into Catalina because it was a foggy day and I got in on the deserted, rocky side. So I kept my mouth shut, dried my clothes, borrowed a little dough from a fisherman I know there and came across to the mainland."

"But first you charted the spot where she went down because you got the bright idea of salvaging that dough yourself."

"I told you he'd make trouble." The old man spoke to Moore. Al Moore's eyes flickered down and Bingham nodded almost imperceptibly.

Cellini gave no hint that he had noticed anything and said: "When you got to L.A. you told your story to Al Moore because it needed more money than you had, to rent a boat and get diving equipment. Moore, in turn, took in Berenice and Charley Stokes and Tanya. So the five of you stand to gain sixty grand by laying out a few thousand?"

"Sure," said Al Moore, "but there's nothing really crooked about it. The guy who owned the dough is dead and besides he probably stole it."

Al Moore went on, talking rapidly, trying to engage Cellini's attention. Randolph Bingham bent over casually, to tie a shoelace. As he did so, his fingers stole toward the edge of a throw rug under Cellini's chair.

"You can stop talking, Moore," said Cellini. The automatic was leveled over his knee. "And you, Bingham, can leave your shoelace untied."

"You're crazy," laughed Moore unsteadily. "We didn't—"

"Shut up. Just tell me why the Coast Guard or some other agency hasn't gotten the idea of sending divers down to look for the *Periwinkle*."

"They don't know where she went down. Only the general area. Besides you saw the date on the paper that printed the story."

"December eight. What of it?"

"It was right after Pearl Harbor and an item like the *Periwinkle* wasn't paid much attention in all the excitement. And that's just the trouble why we can't start diving operations. It's hard to assemble materials and the Coast Guard or Navy would check to see what we're doing. We have to wait a while."

"That's ducky," said Cellini. "You two sit where you are for a few minutes." He backed out.

SUDDENLY, CELLINI SMITH had realized where the murder of a reporter fitted in with the sinking of the *Periwinkle*. And at the same moment, he knew the name of the murderer. He thought of calling Haenigson and tying up the case but it was after two in the morning and he was tired. A few hours could make no difference but it would make Haenigson run around that much longer.

He reached his apartment building and was about to pull to the curb—when he decided to keep going. His mind was changed by a prowl car parked at the front entrance. As he passed the building he could see its side through the rear-view mirror. There was a light in his apartment. The police were waiting to pick him up.

This then was what Berenice Stokes had meant when she had said that he would yet be sorry. She had become panicky at the thought of being booked for the murder of her ex-sweetheart, James Holland. She had decided to jeopardize her share in the sixty grand and had run to the police with her story.

Cellini circled the block several times, then stopped at an all-night drugstore and phoned Homicide. He was informed that Detective-sergeant Ira Haenigson had left. Cellini had a coffee and headed for Haenigson's home. The Homicide man wasn't even waiting for him to be brought in. He had simply ordered the arrest and would take his own sweet time before deigning to prefer charges.

He arrived at the detective-sergeant's house a few minutes later and leaned against the doorbell. It was a very hostile Haenigson, clad in sleazy bathrobe, who opened the door. Cellini stepped inside.

"You found I had a call to pick you up," said the Homicide man without preface, "and you're here to crawl."

"I don't know what you're talking about," replied Cellini brightly. "I just came to give you two hundred bucks that Berenice Stokes stole from the body of Jim Holland."

"Oh, no you don't, Smith. You're caught this time and you can't weasel your way out of it. Withholding evidence."

Cellini snapped his fingers. "Say, I'll bet Berenice spilled it to you. She's the one who stole it, not me. I just took it from her, trying to crack the case."

"That argument and a ration card couldn't get you an ounce

of sugar. There are duly constituted authorities to handle such evidence." He reached for the phone.

"Don't get stuffy, Haenigson. You're just going out of your way to get my license."

"Exactly."

"Then before you make your call, think of how you'll appear when the D.A. talks to me."

"I'll appear in a blue serge suit, Smith—in mourning for you." Haenigson dialed.

"And for yourself because I'll be telling the D.A. who murdered James Holland."

Slowly, the phone was shoved back in its place. Haenigson knew Cellini too well to think he was lying.

"A deal?" asked Cellini. "I know you can crack it but it'll probably take you another few days. Everybody will think you framed me because I cracked the case before you and there will be indignant editorials and I'll be a martyred hero."

"You don't scare me."

"Yes, I do."

"I suppose so," admitted the Homicide man heavily. "I guess it has to be a deal."

"Fine but squeeze the vinegar out of your puss. You know damned well the only reason I held on to that two hundred was to beat you to the punch. Suppose we get the gang together. That Russian carhop, the Stokes couple and a pair called Bingham and Moore. They probably still have their heads together figuring out ways to scare me. You can have them brought here, or better still—we'll mix business with pleasure and visit Tanya."

THIS TIME, TANYA wore a negligee that Cellini found satisfactorily revealing. She allowed the two men to enter and nodded toward Ira Haenigson with sleep-heavy eyes.

"I expected you back, Cellini, but you are not a very brave man to bring help. Or did you bring a lawyer for weetness?"

"This gentleman, Tanya, is a sergeant of the Homicide Bureau."

"Ah. So you try to sell Tanya out for her—"

"Her cute little blackmail racket? No, there are other departments to handle that. The sergeant's just interested in finding out who killed James Holland."

"Hot damn," breathed the carhop.

"I suppose, Haenigson, that Berenice has told you the story of the sixty grand buried at the bottom of the Pacific."

"That's right."

"Then we don't have to go over it," said Cellini. "Randolph Bingham survived the sinking and came back with a chart and a newspaper clipping to prove it and the bright idea of fishing up the dough. He got hold of Alfred Moore who believed his story but Moore couldn't or wasn't prepared to finance the thing by himself. So he asked Tanya to come in on it. He knew Tanya had dough because he was feeding her with twelve bucks' worth of blackmail himself, every month, to pay for wild oats. Or perhaps only one oat, if I know Tanya."

"Please!" The Russian drew herself up with all the haughtiness the negligee allowed. "You said you come here to discover the murderer of Holland so do not discuss agriculture."

"Temper, temper," cooed Cellini. "At any rate, they still wanted more financing so Tanya asked Berenice and her husband to come in and they did. Including Bingham, that made a five-way split netting about twelve grand for each, less expenses. And the five made as pretty a batch of specimens as you'd find any place."

The apartment's door opened and a couple of plainclothesmen ushered in Randolph Bingham, Alfred Moore and Berenice and Charley Stokes. They all seemed sufficiently frightened not to bring up their constitutional rights.

Berenice poked a finger in Cellini's direction and said to Haenigson: "That's the crook who stole the two hundred from Holland. What do you want from us?"

"Shut up," said her husband.

Cellini nodded. "I second that and I'll get to the two centuries in a little while. I was saying what an inspiring crew you are. Randolph Bingham, a sailor who has his boat sunk under him and figures out a way to make dough from it. Berenice, a carhop who can bring you a cheese sandwich or fiddle inside a corpse's clothes for money."

"I didn't kill him!"

"Then there's Berenice's jealous husband—the chef—who threatens people with meat cleavers and who probably knew of his wife's relationship with Holland. Those two probably sank their life's savings into this venture. And Alfred Moore with a nagging wife and a blissful memory of Tanya. His wife must have money or he wouldn't have married her and that's probably the money he used for this scheme and even for Tanya's blackmail."

"It's none of your damned business," Moore snarled.

"Then I'm right. You saw your chance in this to make an easy fortune and leave your wife. In fact, you got to the point where you weren't satisfied with just twelve grand as your share.

You didn't know how you'd do it but you decided to scare Berenice and her husband out of the thing and you hired me with instructions to snoop around to see what I could find. But before you could figure out how to get rid of them, Holland was murdered and you became frightened. You knew that if this thing got into the open, you'd never get the dough from the *Periwinkle*, so you told me a lot of half-truths and tried to keep me busy with phoney assignments. Is that right?"

Moore didn't reply.

"Then we get to Tanya," Cellini continued. "Here's an artist at blackmail who isn't too greedy. She has this apartment and keeps working at the drive-in where she can show her legs and hook more suckers. She even lassoed her boss."

"But you, of course, are wonderful." Tanya's voice oozed sarcasm. "We are all beasts except you. You are perfect."

"I DON'T CLAIM to be perfect," said Cellini. "The only reason I'm mentioning it is because you wouldn't find many in the country who'd act like this bunch."

"What are you getting at?" asked the Homicide man.

"The date the *Periwinkle* was supposed to go down. December eight. This bunch saw their opportunity there. They figured the country was busy with other things besides bothering about a yacht that sank and they thought they could take advantage of it. I don't like that kind of thing."

"I don't think I like it either," said Haenigson.

"Good, because I want you to throw the book at them."

Old Man Bingham spoke. "You can't get me on nothing."

"Really? How long have you been a sailor?"

"Thirteen years."

"You're a liar," said Cellini flatly. "Where are your discharge papers or even your union card?"

"I lost 'em in the sinking."

"That sinking was a cute story. How did it tell?"

"We was going pretty fast with the wind behind us and we got into a heavy following sea—"

"That's memorized nicely," said Cellini, "but it's a mistake to use the same words every time. I don't know anything about the sea but even I knew you were a phoney when you told me that you were standing on the prow."

"What's wrong with it?"

"A real sailor would never say he stood on the prow. He'd use the word *bow*."

Al Moore sat up straight. "You mean we fell for a racket?"

"That's right. The nearest this guy ever got to water was in a whiskey chaser. There never was any *Periwinkle*. You fell for a gag that kept him in clover. You gave him twelve hundred bucks to rent a fishing tub that only cost four hundred and he pocketed the difference. All of you probably kept lending him money and you told me, Moore, that he got two hundred from you the other day."

"But what about that newspaper item about the sinking?" demanded Berenice Stokes plaintively.

"That's where the murder of the reporter, Jim Holland, comes in. Since he was a reporter, I connected him with that newspaper story. That was the only way to connect him—that and the two hundred dollars Moore gave to Bingham. Bingham gave his money to Holland and later Berenice stole it from Holland's body. I figured that this money Bingham gave to Holland was bribery. The reporter came around to the drive-in to visit Berenice and recognized Bingham who used to hang around there. Bingham gave the money to Holland and told him to forget him and go away. But, like Oliver Twist, Holland came back for more. Whether it was for more Berenice or more bribery I don't know but he was killed by Bingham who was afraid his nice racket would be ruined."

The gun Ira Haenigson had leveled at Randolph Bingham kept him from moving but his eyes blazed at Cellini.

"The reporter recognized Bingham," Cellini continued, "because they both worked on the same paper from which that item about the sinking came—the *Standard*—and if you'll call them they'll probably tell you that Holland used to work there."

"He did," said the detective-sergeant.

"I thought so. But Bingham wasn't a reporter. He worked on the presses and on the late afternoon of December seventh they were turning out the early Monday editions. Then the news came on Pearl Harbor and the presses were stopped right where they were and the idea for the racket was born in Bingham's mind. He pulled out some of these incompleted papers from the stopped presses. He probably knows something about printing and linotyping and in one corner of the page he stuck in that yarn about the *Periwinkle* sinking with him. He probably spent a few days carefully hand-setting the thing. That's how he got his bait for the suckers."

Charley Stokes leaped to his feet. "That dirty chiseler!"

"I want to settle something with you." Cellini grabbed the chef and dragged him into the bathroom. "Now how about that ten bucks you owe me, Charley? You lost it in a fair bet and if I don't get it I'll stick your head in the bowl and flush the thing."

He got it.